Alexander Hazard

And The Mysterious Orb

The Unseen, The Unknown, The Mysterious,

The Legends And Myths.

For Without Imagination Nothing Exists,

With Imagination Everything Is Possible.

C.M. Couper

DEDICATIONS,

*In loving memory of my long departed Grandmother
Whom I cherished with all my heart and soul.
Elsie Pearl Amaral*

*My dear departed Father who left my
world sooner than I wished.
I love you so very much.
Wayne Edward Couper*

*Most importantly my Mother for without her this novel would
never have been possible.
She has guided me throughout my life and has been there for me when no one
else was. I would not be here right now without her.
My Mother created my imagination and for that I will always be
grateful for the rest of my life.
I love you Mother! With All My Heart and Soul!
Gloria Jean Couper*

Contents

Chapter 1. Home

One very early morning just outside Dublin, a young twelve-year-old boy stood barefooted in the archway of his parents' cream sandstone home. Alex was gazing down the hallway with his light blue eyes. His short wavy auburn hair was unbrushed and messy, his pale blue buttoned shirt that hung on his back was wrinkled and aged along with his wrinkled black pants.

Alex looked dishevelled as he watched his father through the set of large glass doors that sealed off the inventing room at the end of the hallway.

His father worked tirelessly day in and day out, inside that inventing room. In fact, he worked so much that Alex sometimes had forgotten what his father's voice sounded like. Only on the rare occasion, Alex would see his father William poke his head out and yell, "I'm so close, so close Ethna. I can feel it. I can feel it in my bones! Alex never knew what his father meant. He only knew that it must have been exciting news as anytime his father had yelled this out, he had big bright eyes and a huge smile. However, by the next day, the excitement had drained entirely away from his father's face. The truth of the matter was William had been yelling those same words out those glass doors for almost three years now . To be exact, it had been two years and five months, not that Alex was counting or anything. He knew this because, any spare time Alex had, he would stand in that archway, hoping to hear his father yelling out with excitement that he had finally finished the project he was working on.

Alex continued to gaze through the closed glass doors, looking at all the unusual items and bits and pieces lying around. He could see a tall wooden ladder leaning against half-empty Bookshelves, as most of the Books lay scattered across the floor. In the corner, on top of a small round wooden table, was an old world globe. In the centre of the room stood a large blackboard with a wooden frame.

Squinting his eyes, Alex struggled to see what his father had written on the board. A rather odd feeling came over Alex as he noticed strange symbols written in chalk. He had never seen this type of writing before. Alex looked away from the board to see a few wooden chairs, one of which lay on the floor and another against an old ornate carved desk. A microscope, quill, ink and a rolled-out parchment lay with a lit oil lantern. It was casting a dim yellowish glow, giving the whole room quite an eerie feeling.

Ethna, William's wife, a thin woman with blond shoulder-length hair, walked past Alex wearing a green leaf-patterned dress covered by a white apron. She was carrying a metal tray with two pieces of dry bread and a mug of broth. Ethna turned her head to look at Alex giving him a big smile. Although Alex could see her smile, he could also see into the depths of her tearful eyes the truth of her feelings that she was trying to hide, the sorrow, the sadness of lost dreams and lost hope. Ethna had been a nervous wreck since the day William started his new project. Just by the way he looked at the astrology and alchemy symbols on the parchment and blackboard as if he had found a chest of gold, Ethna knew that until William had solved the puzzle, he would be consumed entirely. Until then, it would be an all-consuming mystery. Ever since William began his new project, the family bank had run dry. The food was scarce, and the bills were never paid on time. With William no longer being able to support his family, Alex had been forced to give up his schooling early and his mother sent him to work using the skills grandfather Fergus Hazard had taught him before his passing. A carpenter by trade, Fergus would take young Alex along with him at every available opportunity, knowing full well that he was getting older and would not always be there to help the family. Thereby taking Alex with him, the town folk would grow to know the boy and so when the sad day came of Fergus's passing many of the people came to show their respect to the kindly hard-working old fellow.

As time moved on and without grandfather's financial help, it became apparent to Ethna that Alex would no longer be able to continue with any schooling. She knew that the kind-hearted folk around the village would be more than happy to give Alex even the smallest of repair jobs to help provide for his family.

Especially now that the whispers had been spreading around the town that the family had been struggling for so long.

Everyone knew that Alex was an exceptionally intelligent boy and had the mind and skills way beyond his age where anything he set out to do, anything he wanted to learn, he would set his mind to achieving it within a short period. Alex took pride in his work. However, he never let it go to his head, he was kind to all, treated everyone as an equal, no matter if it was a senior woman, a child of three or even a pet dog. Alex knew what it was like to be poor and a little bit different. Being accepted for who you are, was crucial to Alex. He was aware that you must treat people with kindness and respect if you wanted it in return. These thoughts were passing through Ethna's mind of how proud she was of her only son. 'My son, she thought to herself, if only he was still here. I wonder what sort of things he would like? I wonder what he would look like now?' Suddenly, she literately came to a stop, nearly dropping the tray, 'Oh my goodness, I can't think about him right now, Alex needs me.' Snapping herself out of a dream-like state, she continued to walk up to the glass doors and knocked lightly, smiling at her husband, who opened the door a little to pass the tray through.

Alex could see her smile turning into a frown as the tray was passed through the gap. He could see the worry on her face. Ethna noticed new wrinkles on William's face, the darkness surrounding his eyes from lack of sleep as he glanced down at the tray. His long messy brown hair and beard had begun to reveal light shades of tangled grey. He looked up at her and she saw frustration, desperation and desire in his eyes. He smelt like salty sweat, damp clothing and bad breath.

All this saddened her knowing full well what it was that drove her husband to such desperation. She felt the same ache in her heart for him, her son, his son, their son being a well-hidden secret known only to the both of them, the mysterious thing that had happened those long years ago. As Ethna stood there watching her husband through the glass doors, she was remembering those first few months of moving to Dublin. When William was a strong young newly married man, with big dreams of being able to have his very own inventing room, where he could carry out his experiments - the profound changes he would make for the betterment of mankind.

'We were all happy back then,' she thought to herself, 'until that fateful morning when he, our baby, went missing. He was so little, and I will never see him ever again. Alex can never know, well best not to think on that right now. I must hold myself together for the boy.'

As Ethna turned, she was startled to find Alex standing right in front of her, tears had begun to trickle down Ethna's cheeks as Alex moved over to put his arm around her.

"I know mother, I understand," said Alex. She looked up at him and kissed his forehead thinking 'you will never know son' and then slowly tottered off down the hallway with her head in her hands trying to hide the tears.

Alex took one last look through the door, watching his father flop into the seat, scoffing down the food while looking through a microscope. Being totally oblivious to Alex even being there, let alone watching him hurriedly writing with quill and ink onto the piece of light brown parchment on the desk. Alex turned away, grabbing his hat and wooden carry box of tools and left for work.

The next morning Alex awoke to his mother's call, "Alex! Breakfast! You better hurry or you will be late to fix Mr and Mrs Bulbidge's cupboard before they go to the garden market today!" Alex knew it would be the same breakfast, as usual, a small bowl of leftover porridge from yesterday's breakfast. He walked out of his bedroom and into the archway to see his father when all of a sudden Alex noticed his father throwing his food onto a piece of parchment. Looking bright-eyed and exhilarated, Alex saw his father run over to a Bookshelf grabbing something, then running over to the door poking his head out, "Don't just stand there, boy!!! COME NOW!!" Coming back to reality, he shouted out "Coming Father!" and then ran down the hallway pushing the glass doors open. It was like a dream. He had never been able to set foot inside the inventing room his whole life,

"Father! What is it?" he asked excitedly, given that he knew it would be something crucial.

"Put on your coat, we are going forthwith!"

Alex ran out to the front door, grabbing his brown overcoat off the hat and coat stand and pulled it on.

William walked up to the stand, pulled off his black hat, put it on his head and grabbed his black overcoat, threw it over himself as he quickly walked outside. Alex followed his father out to the chestnut brown draft horses and cart. William seized the reins and with a swift flick, the draft horses reared up and galloped as fast as their legs could over the rolling highlands with lush green grass, down the dirt and pebbled roads and into town.

In town, there were people everywhere. Some were casually strolling, some thundering along trying to get to wherever they were going, some just pacing up and down the streets and buying vegetables from the market stalls. People were singing and playing instruments with money being dropped into hats and bowls in front of them.

William turned to look at Alex and forced a small round object into his hand, "Here, take this. Put it in your pocket son and show no one. You understand me...? Understand me, Alex? This is of great importance that no one should see this object."

"I understand," replied Alex, with grave concern showing on his face as he stepped out of the cart,

"Don't mess this up, now go... go straight to Professor Yen 'Niles' Cottage and don't look back."

"Yes, Father."

"Oh, and one more thing..., don't go anywhere near Stonehenge. I am trusting you to guard this with your life. Don't come back until it is done," and with a flick of the reins, William was gone.

Alex looked around and noticed he was standing in front of a large ship and a chubby man wearing a white uniform trimmed with blue and wearing a matching hat.

"Ticket, please."

"Uhh," replied Alex.

"Well... Where is it? Hand it to me, stop wasting my time."

"I... don't have one, Sir."

"Well get out of the way then," replied the man, as another man came from behind Alex pushing him out of the way. Alex stood there rummaging through his pockets, "No money, what do I do now?" he said to himself. "Father would be so angry if I returned home."

Looking around, he spotted a man sitting in an old wooden yawl next to a long wooden dock.

'It's worth a shot,' he thought to himself. Alex made his way up the dock towards the yawl.

"Excuse me, Sir?"

The man looked up slowly, brushing aside his long wavy brown hair from his dark green eyes, an ugly scar covered the whole right side of his face. The man quickly put his head back down covering the scar,

"What, is it, boy?" he asked slowly in a deep voice.

"I was just wondering if you could take me across the water, Sir?"

"Maybe... for a price."

"I... I don't have any money."

"A very nice watch you have there." The man rolled his eyes upwards at a small silver pocket watch with engravings of dragons and runes, that was hanging out of Alex's overcoat pocket. It must have fallen out during the bumpy ride into town.

"It was my grandfathers," Alex replied.

The man stared at Alex through his tangled straw-like hair.

"I really don't want to part with it."

The man continued to stare. Alex looked down at his watch, thinking about how important it was to get to where he was going. He took the watch off and held it in his hand. "However..., I suppose I could always find another one, one day," said Alex, thinking he would be most unlikely to come across another the same.

Alex put on a brave face, "Would you take my watch as payment?"

The man nodded. Alex held it out to the man. "Please look after it," he said, pleading as the man grabbed the watch like it was a treasure. "Of course, get in." He gestured for Alex to sit on a wooden seat and then grabbed a dark blue velvet cloth out of his tattered old bag, wrapped the watch inside it, then quickly shoved it into his bag.

Chapter 2. The Journey

A bright blue sky, soft white fluffy clouds with the sun lightly shining through, a cool breeze blowing over his face, while the water was rippling beside the yawl as it glided through the water. Alex felt he was in heaven, no houses, buildings, trees, pathways or grass, just the beauty of the open sea. He put his hand down the side of the yawl and touched the streaming water with the tip of his fingers, "I wouldn't do that if I were you."

"Why not?" asked Alex, as he felt something solid and slippery in the water. "Ah! What was that?" he shrieked while quickly pulling his fingers out of the water and looking down beside the boat. He saw a vast dark shadow following alongside them.

"Hush now… you don't want to frighten her."

"Frighten who? Or What?"

"Bessie…,"

"What? Who is Bessie?"

"You've never heard of the Loch Ness?"

"Well… Yes, that's a myth, this isn't the loch… and isn't the loch ness monster supposed to be in the loch?"

"Yes... And no. Who's to say there is merely one? And she is not a monster... she is more of a pet..., a pet kitten or... a puppy." A small light grey head peeked out of the water, followed by an exceptionally long neck.

"Ah!" yelled Alex jumping to the other side of the boat, making the boat rock from side to side.

"That's no puppy! Or kitten!"

"Shush now. Don't scare her... she won't hurt you. Think yourself lucky. She generally doesn't come out when there's a stranger around."

"Scare her? Lucky?" said Alex, as the head came closer and licked the side of his face "Ewe, gross... Loch Ness slobber." It then started sniffing around his pants pocket.

"Bessie... Bessie... Leave the boy alone," said the man, trying to shoo her away from him.

Alex held his pocket tight so that Bessie didn't knock the object into the water. Bessie put her head up and let out a little whimper and started whining.

"What do you have there? What the devil do you have in your pocket?"

"Nothing. It's nothing... Just uh..." Then Bessie gave Alex a big nudge with her nose, almost pushing him out of the boat and into the water. The water was splashing into the boat. Alex was holding on tightly so as to not fall out.

"Fine... here. Take this...," said the man, as he plunged his hand into a bucket that was covered with an old rag, pulling out a large fish and throwing it into the water.

Bessie popped her head up fast and dived splashing into the water after the fish. The boat rocked sideways dangerously, as the water started splashing massively into the boat.

"Just be still boy!" the man yelled out to Alex as he grabbed an empty bucket that was now rolling around the deck of the boat. He started to scoop up the water and throw it overboard.

Once the water had all been scooped out, Alex sat there thinking about how strange this was and that he will have an excellent story to tell his family when he gets home. They sat quietly; there was no sound except for the birds flying over the sea and the sound of the waves splashing against the side of the boat.

When they reached the shore, Alex grabbed hold of an old bollard and stepped out of the yawl and onto an old wooden wharf. The man stretched his arm out, with his hand high in the air as a quick wave and yelled out "Be seeing ya boy!" and sailed off into the distance. Alex thought to himself, 'I hope I never see him again!' Searching around the trees, bushes and shrubs, Alex found a stone pathway heading east. Pushing the shrubs aside as he stepped onto the trail, Alex looked at his pocket and remembered that his watch had gone. He glanced at the sky, it was getting dark.

Alex said to himself, 'I better start looking for a place to lay down.'

As he walked further, Alex noticed a small broken down cart on the side of the pathway. 'This will do the job nicely,' he said climbing into the old broken down cart, lying down, curling up, hugging his knees and falling asleep.

Bright light, the sound of children giggling, a lute playing and people singing, Alex opened his eyes. Children were looking over the cart giggling at him. He tried jumping to his feet, however, was unsuccessful and instead fell on his bottom with a THUMP!

With one of his legs slipping through a hole that was made when a wooden plank had broken in half, a loud, deep laugh was heard over the children.

"HaHa Come on! Out of the way, little ones!" Alex tried pulling out his leg but failing. "Hold on, boy, let me help you!" A massive, giant man came forward shooing the children away. The man grabbed Alex by the shoulders and with a quick pull, Alex was out and standing on the ground.

"Uh..., thanks... Sir," replied Alex, looking up at the large, tall and broad man who wore a white buttoned top, tan trousers, had shoulder-length dark brown hair and looked very well shaven.

"That's ok young man, what's your name?"

"I, I am, Alex, Sir."

"No need to call me Sir... young one, you can call me Wayne," the man said happily with a broad smile on his face.

"Yes Sir, I mean, Wayne."

"I bet you haven't eaten yet, have you young Alex?"

"No, not yet."

"You don't seem to have anything with you either, that's ok, come, walk with me and we will remedy that and put some food in your belly and music in your ears," Alex followed Wayne, passing children playing and to a campfire with a large pot of what looked like bubbling stew. The smell was making Alex's mouth water.

A few men and women were surrounding the fire singing. One boy who looked like he was about the same age as Alex with short dark brown hair, white top and tan coloured trousers was playing a lute.

All went quiet as Wayne and Alex approached the fire. A thin, rather tall lady with long blond hair, wearing a light blue dress looked up at them and said, "So who's this young one?"

"This is Alex," replied Wayne, as he sat on a large log that surrounded the fire. The wood made a deep groaning cracking sound.

"Ah I see, Sarah, please get Alex a bowl of our lovely stew and a nice warm cup of tea."

A girl who also looked about the same age as Alex walked out from behind a shrub, carrying a basket with berries inside. She was a little taller than Alex, had light brown hair in two pigtails and was wearing a beautiful light pink dress. Alex could not believe his eyes, she was the prettiest girl he had ever seen in his entire life.

"This is Sarah and Jonathan," the lady pointed to the girl and boy. As the girl got closer to the boy, Alex realised they must be twins as they looked very much alike.

"And I am Tabitha."

"Nice to meet you," replied Alex.

"Oh, look here Wayne, we have a polite gentleman in our presence. It's so nice to see young men like you still exist. Now come sit by me while Sarah gets you some of this delicious stew we have here."

"Yes, Mam."

"Oh, dear sweet boy, no need to call me Mam. You may just call me Tabitha. Come now, come make yourself at home and share our warm fire, it is an icy morning."

Alex nodded and took a seat on the log next to Tabitha.

"So, where are you from Alex? I've got to say I've never seen you around this neck of the woods before," asked Tabitha.

"I come from Dublin."

"Wow, that's a long way. What makes you come all the way over here?"

Alex wondered to himself what he should and shouldn't say "I... I."

"That's ok," she smiled at him. "Everyone has secrets. There is no need to say anything. You seem like a sweet boy and that's all that matters to us."

Alex nodded as he was handed a large plate of warm stew. The boy played the lute. His sister sang and everyone joined in the chorus. That day seemed to fly past. Alex had the time of his life, helping Sarah pick berries, learning how to play the lute, learning new songs. Everyone there was so friendly. Alex felt like he fitted right in.

Chapter 3. Predestinate

When Alex awoke the next morning, he was nice and warm from sleeping next to the fire. He sat up slowly as he looked around. People were walking around packing up their things. A loud, deep voice came from behind him.

"Ar I see you're awake there lad, we will be heading off shortly. My wife and I had a little chat this morning and we figured that we may need some help on our way. Where is it you were off to?"

"Uhh. Just past Stonehenge, Sir."

"I see. Well, we will be travelling through there if you would like to join our troop. You are quite welcome to come along, as long as you don't mind doing a few jobs here and there of cause."

"Oh... I would love to. Yes please, Sir."

"Remember, no need to call me Sir, in our troop, we treat each person the same as the next person. There is no leader, just everyone hitching up their britches and helping out."

"Yes..., yes Wayne. I will be sure to do my fair share. I may be young. However, I have a lot of skills you may put to use."

"Well, here you go," said Wayne, handing Alex a few things to take into the wagon. "That's a good start young lad," said Wayne, pointing over to a large green and gold painted Gypsy wagon.

After everything was packed Wayne and Tabitha climbed into the front of the wagon. Alex, Sarah and Jonathan all sat on a thin silky patterned material that was lying on the floor in the back of the wagon and Sarah got out a deck of cards. "Anyone for cards?" she asked.

Sarah shuffled the cards and began to deal them out. Inside the wagon was one large bed at the end, portioned off by thick velvet purple curtains. On the left side of the wagon was one single bed on top of another. The same was on the right and in the middle was where the three sat and played cards. "So what age are you Alex?" asked Sarah.

"I am twelve and you?"

"Ahhhh...," She said. "I thought you were older. I am normally good at guessing ages. My brother and I are fifteen."

"Yeah, a lot of people think I am older than I am. What do you do Jonathan?"

"You can call me Jon. I do some work for our troop, like playing the lute for each town we stop in so that we can make some extra money on our travels. Some of our troop do stage performances, juggling, fire-throwing, things like that. What sort of stuff did you do Alex?"

"Well. I did some carpentry, gardening and a few odd jobs in our village." The twins looked at him shocked. Jon was sitting with his mouth open and said, "Carpentry? Wow... and you say you are twelve?"

"Yes, I am, but a lot of people say I seem older, not sure why though, to me, I'm just... me...,"

"But that's just Brilliant! Do other people your age do things like that too?"

"No, not really, most just do garden work or helping out in the kitchens."

"Brilliant," replied Jon, "The most exciting thing I get to do is help dad polish his swords."

"Oh wow, your dad has swords?" asked Alex, excitedly.

"Yep, dad is so proud of his swords."

The wagon stopped quickly. Everything on the wall shelving toppled over onto the three. they were trying to keep themselves balanced so as to not hit their head on something. The sound of frightened horses surrounded them, and they could hear people yelling out at each other.

"What's going on?" said Alex, startled.

"I don't know. This hasn't happened before," replied Jon, looking troubled.

The whole wagon started shaking like there was an earthquake. There was light pulsing all around them changing from brown, white, red, blue, brown, white, red, blue. The light was so bright, they had to squint their eyes to see anything - brown, white, red, blue, brown, white, red, blue. The lights got brighter and brighter. There was a loud low humming sound.

All Alex could think to himself was 'please, stop, please stop.' All of a sudden, the lights vanished. Everything went still. The three stared at each other. Jon opened and closed his mouth, swallowing a few times trying to bring moisture to his very dry and parched throat and said, "What the hell was that?"

Sarah just sat there shaking her head. Alex looked at them both wondering what they should do then said, "Listen, listen." They all went quiet.

"What? I don't hear anything," replied Jon.

"Exactly."

"What do you mean?" asked Sarah.

"What's missing? What don't we hear?"

"Our Troop!" said Sarah and Jon frantic at the same time. They both stood up quickly and ran outside. Alex stood there wondering what to do, then heard Sarah and Jon calling out names. Alex felt something pulsing like a heartbeat on his thigh. At first, he thought it was just his nerves. He looked down and saw his pocket throbbing. Alex put his hand inside his pocket and yanked out the orb, throwing it on the ground.

"Ah!" shrieked Alex as he clutched his hand. It was so hot he felt like he had placed his hand on top of a stove that had been left on high for hours. He glanced at his hand cradling it and there was nothing, no mark, no nothing. He looked down at the orb and noticed it was glowing dull, brown, white, red, blue, brown, white, red, blue, then stopped.

He stared at it not knowing what to do, then looked back at his hand realising it was no longer hurting, He pointed his index finger and slowly guided it towards the orb, and touched it. He flinched pulling back his hand. However, it was no longer hot. Alex reached down to the ground picking up the orb and looked at it. Footsteps were heard, so Alex quickly shoved the orb back into his pocket. Jon ran inside, looking upset "It's… it's…," stuttered Jon.

"It's what?"

"It's mum and dad and everyone… even the horses… come look!" Then he ran back outside. Alex got up and followed Jon. "Uh," said Alex in shock as he stepped out of the wagon and looked around. There was what seemed to be dead people lying around on the ground. The horses were still connected to the carts but looked as though they had collapsed. As Alex looked closer, he realised they were not dead at all.

"They are breathing!" he yelled out, spotting the twins leaning over their mum and dad trying to wake them up. Alex looked around at the trees that were surrounding them. "Where are we?" he said to himself as he began to walk around the bodies seeing if anyone was awake. He then pushed his way through a large shrub and walked through some leafy trees shaped into an arch. There was a clearing with bright green grass, small white flowers and large grey stones in a circle, "St.., St.., Stonehenge, how did we get here?" Alex stuttered, rubbing his arms for warmth as he felt a freezing cold breeze swoop past him. Walking closer to the stones a strange feeling come over Alex, a sense of someone close to him had died. "What's wrong with me? What's going on?" Feeling sad, trying to ignore it, he walked closer. Tears were forming in his eyes. As Alex walked into the middle of the circle, a dark mist was developing around him, making it hard to see. It was getting dark and cold. Alex felt something crawling on his arm. He flinched and shook it. A spider was tapping its prickly long hairy legs quickly up his arm.

"Get off! GET OFF!" he yelled. Another spider began to crawl up his leg, another up his back, another on his chest and another and another and another. They were all crawling up and around his body, their long legs were tapping fast on his skin, on his back and behind his neck,

"GET OFFF!!..." Alex was flicking them off, in clusters with his hands. For every one that Alex managed to get off; it seemed twice as many came back. He felt tingles all over himself, everything was going blurry and fading. He fell to his knees, put his head in his hands and closed his eyes. Then... Nothing. It was quiet. It felt like the spiders had gone; he slowly opened his eyes and stood up. Alex looked at his hands "Oh my...," He looked at his arms and legs, "Oh my!" His whole body was covered in a transparent webbing that was glowing brown, white, red, blue. There was a loud crack of thunder. He jumped as fork lightning struck the stones.

Fires blazed around them. A soft rain began to trickle down with the fire still burning. The ground under him formed puddles of water. A snap cold wind blew over him. He shivered. The puddles crackled as they iced over. Alex was going blue. His body freezing, he put his arms around himself to stay warm. The rain turned into snow. Everything turned white. Alex couldn't see Stonehenge anymore, only snow and dead trees. A thick mist swirled around him making a high pitch whistle. It was growing bigger, forming a giant orb around him. All of a sudden, Alex was raised fast up in the air, like a flash of lightning in the sky. He stopped completely, screaming as he fell like a meteorite. Then THUMP! he hit the ground.

Chapter 4. Humbletin

Lying sprawled out on his back, Alex slowly opened his eyes. Feeling numb from head to toe, he slowly moved thinking it would be painful… except it wasn't. Looking at his arms and legs, he noticed they were back to normal, no more webbing. He then looked around at what was unknown faces of people surrounding him.

There were whispers. "Is he ok?" asked a woman. "Who is he?"

"Where did he come from?"

"Once before."

"Only ever once before."

"Last time was a little boy."

"Is it the same thing?"

"Who is he?"

"How did you get here boy?" a man's voice said out loud,

"I…" he looked around trying to figure out where he was. All he could see was the light grey pathway. He was now surrounded by a group of people; one woman was wearing all black with a dark blue cloak, another a blue velvet long dress, one man was dressed in a suit, another was wearing a long dark brown robe with a hood.

"I..., where, where am I?" asked Alex, rubbing his head as he looked up at a moderately tall, skinny man with ginger hair and an exceptionally large nose. "Humbletin, of course" he laughed.

"Wah?" Alex wrinkled his face, bemused.

"Humbletin..." The man replied.

Alex rubbed his head again, still feeling befuddled, "You do know Humbletin? Right?" asked the man.

"I've..., I've never heard of it," said Alex, looking from face to face seeing if he recognised anyone there from the troop. The man looked at him with curiosity in his eyes.

"Do you know what your name is?"

"Alex"

"Well, it's nice to meet you Alex" The man stood up straight, brushed off his dark green vest, tucked his white undershirt into his dark green long pants and said, "Well... my name is Frank McKormick, High Qualified Herbalist of Humbletin. Always ready for any situation that arises. Capable of curing anything put in my way; wobbly crinkle wrinkles, slippery shaking shingles, floppy flaking fingers, garbled marbled bubble gums, gastro...,".

"Yes, yes, yes Frank. I think the boy is suffering from a slight problem of memolossity," said a big pudgy man, standing next to Frank with black hair balding in the middle and front. "You really think so?" asked Frank.

"Yes, I do, and he can't take it all in, by the looks of it." Frank tilted his head sideways looking at Alex, who was still looking from face to face.

"Hmm… Jon, I think you may be right. Well, either way, we can't stay here, I believe it would be best for all if I take this boy under my wing, at least until he gets some of his memories back."

"I do remember…."

"Then where do you live dear boy?" asked Frank.

"Ireland."

"Ireland? Never heard of it. Is it some kind of sub suburb of Humbletin? Have you heard of it, Jon?"

"Nope never in my days have I ever heard of such a place."

"Of course, there is! It's just on the other side of the sea, something happened, and I ended up here! Near Stonehenge and the troop! I have to go back and make sure they are all ok! They were asleep, well, I thought they were dead, but they were just sleeping and…,"

"Stop. Stop dear boy," said Frank.

"Stonehenge, troop, people dead… this is getting worse by the second, Frank."

Jon said looking puzzled.

"Yes… there is no time to waste, Alex, stand up, brush yourself off and come with me."

"Go with you where? I have things to do, places to be, I can't just...,"

"To my house, I will introduce you to my family."

"No... What? No... I can't. I... I have something to do. Something important to do. I must...,"

"I'm sorry son, but it will just have to wait," replied Frank. "I'm not your son, I have to go."

"I... I didn't mean it that way, just come with me boy, no need to make a scene."

"What are you all looking at? We are not here for your entertainment!" said Jon, to all the surrounding people.

Everyone parted and went their separate ways. You could see them all gossiping to each other.

"People would think this is the main event of the year," said Jon. "

Yes well... only once, now twice," replied Frank.

Alex looked up at Frank with disappointment in his eyes and said, "Ok... I will go with you but... I have something I have to do, and I won't be staying."

"Yes! Let's leave it at that shall we," said Frank.

"I'll see you later Frank, keep me updated on the boy, will you?" asked Jon.

"Indeed...," replied Frank.

Jon smiled, waved and went on his way leaving Frank and Alex by themselves.

Alex stood up and had a better look around at Humbletin and went a shade of white, "I'm dead."

"Don't be silly boy! You're not dead."

The roads were curvy and made from what looked to be small shiny crystals that mirrored the sky. "I am dead."

"For the last time, you're not dead."

"But the sky, on the road."

"It only does that in the afternoon and night, during the day they are just pebbles."

Alex just stood there not moving with the words going over and over, echoing in his head about what his father had said, 'Don't go anywhere near Stonehenge, near Stonehenge, near Stonehenge.'

Frank looked at him and said, "Humbletin. I suppose I better explain since you can't remem... since... You're not at home that is." Alex looked at Frank in a daze feeling like he was dreaming. A strong smell of cedar wood past his nose. He then turned his head and jumped backwards, almost falling over his own feet.

"Ahh... What is that?" he said, alarmed as a wooden chair walked past following its owner.

"Obviously… it's a chair," laughed a man strolling along with the chair following him.

"Hey Dan, I see you are getting one of your chairs fixed," Frank assumed.

"Sure are, the poor thing has a case of lumpels. It can't stop scratching itself. I'll be having to scrub this one for a week."

"Good luck with that."

"Thanks, I'll be needing it," said the man and continued to walk on.

"Mr," said Alex, still staring at the chair, "Mr McKormick.

"Yes?"

"Why was the chair…,"

"Walking?"

"Umm… Yeah?"

"Don't you remember… What I mean to say is… Don't chairs move where you came from?"

"No…,"

"Well, don't worry, it's just the mist, see the mist around the outside of town?" Frank pointed to a silvery blue mist in the distance that seemed to be slowly moving. It was like a dome around the entire city. Alex looked up. The mist was transparent in the sky. He could only just see the stars, Alex nodded.

"It creates living energy. Some people call it The Sparks of Life. The energy goes into everything inside Humbletin, including our tables, chairs, cups, spoons, even the lamplights over there." Frank pointed to a forest green arched lamplight ahead of them. It was moving. It looked like it was watching over a circular garden of snapdragons and poppies that were underneath it. "They have a dazzling personality. Anyway, let's get a move on before it gets too late, this way!" Frank pointed to his right, along the pathway and started walking ahead of Alex. "Where are we going?"

"To my home, of course, you get the honour of meeting the family." Alex could now see more roads across the land, some turning transparent as they spiralled upwards to large houses above, each on their own cone-shaped portion of land, floating above the houses below.

"Come on Alex! Stop dawdling." Alex realised Frank was halfway up the pathway waiting for him.

"Coming," he replied, walking faster and hoping the houses would not fall on him. "I see you were looking at the houses up there?" asked Frank, as Alex approached him.

"Yeah."

Frank pointed to an enormous window. Alex could see a massive hanging portrait on the wall inside. A woman was walking around. "Most of the people in those houses are prim and proper. If you know what I mean? They have important jobs like Phoenix school teachers, who teach our Phoenix babies, Humbletin astronomy scientists, automobile inventors, one day you could own a house like that Alex if you can...,"

"Remember.?."

"Alex, you have to understand, you have memolossity. I know it's hard to accept it, as you have false memories. The mind is a strange thing, Alex, it will make its own memories when it chooses. You don't know any different because you only know what your brain lets you know."

Alex just stood there listening quietly.

"You will feel unlike yourself for a while. The mind cannot handle not remembering, so it makes its own memories. It's nothing to worry about. You will be back to yourself in no time. Just don't go making any harsh decisions, or you may regret it. I completely understand the way you are feeling.

It will be hard for a while until you do remember. I suggest you take my advice... Go along with things and you never know you might just like it here."

"My father is going to kill me...," said Alex, holding his head in his hands.

"All will work out one way or another, you'll see."

Chapter 5. The Family

"Here we are," said Frank, as they reached a dirt pathway that led to a door of an old, round, slender, tall house, with stairs winding around it to another door with a small cone-shaped roof.

There was a sign next to the pathway with old scriptwriting 'Letter T, number 3 (T/3) of Sutoona Way'. "Nice...," replied Alex, not really knowing what to say. "Thank you. You know our house is one of the longest standing buildings in Humbletin. You wouldn't think so by looking at it, but this house was my mother-in-law's. Sessil passed it down to my wife. She was a lovely old duck. You would have liked her. All the old houses you see here have been passed down, from mother to daughter, father to son, all utmost treasured. They remind us of what's most important in life."

"What is that?"

"Family..., nothing in Humbletin could ever replace or become the same value as family," said Frank, looking up at the house as they arrived at the front door.

"Is it safe?"

Frank laughed, "Safe? Of course. It's made of dark rustic blue wood, from the ancient round tibblebark tree. Amazing trees they were. I wish I had seen one. They were huge, said to have had golden leaves which bestowed magical healing powers to the beholder."

"It has healing powers?"

"Not anymore. People didn't realise by building their homes inside these trees that the golden leaves would never grow again. No one has seen a Tibblebark Tree in centuries."

"They all died?"

"Well... yes. And no. There is a myth that outside Humbletin there are loads, but that's just a myth. You would never want to go out there, you would die." Frank knocked on the front door of the house. They could hear a voice yell out "Come in! The door isn't locked!" Frank opened the door. "You're late! you know I worry about you when you're out so late!" A woman's voice came from another room. "That's my wife, Hazel."

"I'm in the kitchen! Did they keep you back at work again?" They walked into a small round kitchen with lots of pots and pans, some hanging off the roof with herbs hanging to dry, some on shelves with bottled herbs and spices.

Hazel, a medium built woman with curly shoulder-length brown hair, was bending down looking in the oven checking to see if a big chicken was cooked. The smell of rosemary, thyme, honey and chicken was making Alex's mouth water.

"Hazel is the best cook. She has even won trophies from cooking events," said Frank.

"Frank, go get Elsie. She is up in her roo...," She turned around and noticed Alex was there. "Oh, dear boy, I'm terribly sorry, Frank didn't... Frank!" She glared at Frank then continued to say "Why! Why didn't you warn me we had company?" Hazel took off her maroon and baby pink checked cooking mittens, straightened her dark maroon apron and put her hand out to shake Alex's with a big smile on her face and said, "Hi, sweetie I am Hazel, the woman of the house."

"I'm Alex," they shook hands.

"Nice to meet you, Alex, would you like to stay for dinner?"

"Yes please," he replied, with a smile in return, feeling ravenous since he had not eaten since breakfast. "Hazel, there is something I have to tell you," said Frank.

"What is it? You haven't been fired, have you? Oh, pixies and garwinkles! What are we to do? We'll have to sell our cattle, dig into our saving accounts. There won't be any more experiments for you, my dear...,"

"Stop, stop Hazel of course I haven't lost my job."

"Then... then what is it?"

"Alex will be staying with us for a while, He has a case of memolossity."

"Memolossity... that could last for years," replied Hazel.

"Years!" shrieked Alex, his voice cracking slightly. He thought about how angry his father would be by then.

"Don't worry, don't worry... Hazel tends to exaggerate a little, don't you dear," Frank said quickly.

"Oh...., oh, I'm so sorry Alex, silly me, I didn't realise what I was saying. Of course, it may not take that long... You are quite welcome to stay here as long as you like" said Hazel, patting his back.

"Thank you, though I don't intend to stay for long," replied Alex, with a look like he didn't have a choice anyway. All went quiet.

"I'll introduce you to the rest of the family," said Frank, breaking the awkward moment.

"Ok. This way." Frank swung his arm forward like he was going to bowl a bowling ball and pointed in front of him leading Alex out of the kitchen, into the lounge room, up a flight of stairs then knocked on an arched door.

"Elsie are you in there?" asked Frank.

A tall, 11-year-old girl, with short brown hair and freckles, answered the door. "Yes, dad?"

"Elsie this is Alex. He will be staying with us for a while. He has memolossity."

"Hi," said Alex, his voice cracking.

"Hi Alex, welcome to our humble home," she said with a smile.

"I would like it if you could tell him a few things about Humbletin. Maybe you could get Alex to remember where he came from."

"Of cause dad, come on, Alex."

Frank moved aside, let Alex walk past and said, "See you at dinner, Alex." Then left down the stairs.

"Umm. Hi," said a thin girl, with long blond hair tied in a ponytail standing near a window draped with maroon velvet curtains and cream lace.

"Juliana, this is Alex."

"Hi Alex."

"Alex, would you like to see the candles I make? It's a hobby of mine," asked Elsie.

"Sure."

"They're so realistic," said Juliana.

On one of the walls in Elsie's bedroom was a large floor to ceiling cupboard and on the shelves were perfumed candles in all shapes and colours. On the top shelves were wizards' and castles. You could see the great detail that went into them. There was smoke coming out of one of the chimneys in a house, with the light on inside a window. Great wizards were walking around the shelves. One was scratching his head, another was sitting down with his hands on his knees. As they saw Alex, they waved.

Alex thought that if it wasn't for the long wick hanging out of the top of the wizards' pointy hats, they could have passed as real people.

"Like them?" asked Elsie.

"Wow, they are realistic, great!"

"Thanks. I use perfume from the Elfish flowers I buy with money from helping dad in our herb garden out the back. If you stay here long enough, you could help too if you like."

"Sounds good, but... I don't know how long I will be staying."

"I am sure you will love it here." Elsie walked over to a dark rosewood dresser with a big oval mirror. On the dresser was a crystal collection laid out neatly, amethyst, rubies, emeralds, opals, sapphires, a large tigers eye, amongst a variety of other precious stones. There were a few odd-looking purple flowers.

Elsie picked up a flower and held it out to Alex. "Would you like a passionflower, Alex?"

"Uhh..., what for?"

"You eat them. It won't hurt you. The petals are for relaxation. I tend to keep a few around just in case my brother Brandon annoys me, as he usually does. Have you met my brother yet, Alex?" asked Elsie, giving a flower to Juliana and taking one herself. Then sitting on the bed, she picked off a petal and ate it, "Umm... no...,"

"Thank god you haven't. Trust me, you don't want to." Juliana sat on a rosewood rocking chair with a maroon velvet cushion and said, "Elsie your brother is such a big Pratt."

"I know... Sometimes I wonder if Brandon was adopted."

Alex heard a strange knocking sound from the corner of the room. He looked at the high arched roof. There was a skeleton of a pterosaur believed to be an extinct bird, swinging off the ceiling. The bones rippled and knocked together as the wind blew through the window. Something slid and moved a little under his feet. Looking down, he saw a round maroon and cream mat sliding on the polished tibblewood floor. It looked like it was struggling.

"How many times do I have to tell you mat? Stay still!" said Elsie, looking over the bed at the mat.

"It's Ok," said Alex.

"No, it's not really. He does it all the time. What if he does that and I fall over?"

"Stay still," said Alex, pointing at the mat.

Elsie smiled, "You can sit on the bed if you like Alex." Then she fell back onto her soft maroon velvet doona and was enjoying the lovely Sunday afternoon.

Alex sat at the end of the bed. Fresh air was blowing into the room. An ethereal mist of light was shining through the window... 'Thump,' 'Thump,' 'Thump,' footsteps were coming closer to the door, then... stopped.

"Go away Brandon!" yelled Elsie.

An annoying whining sing song came from the other side of the door.

"Oi! Elsie, Elsie, little mousey, open the door or I'll blow it down!"

"No! go away!" She pointed to the door and said, "Lock!" The door locked.

"Open! open! open now!" yelled Brandon. The door handle was shivering in fright.

"That's it! I'm telling mum!" shouted Elsie.

"You tell mum all you like. She won't care!"

'Thump,' thump,' 'thump' "Mum! mum!" They could hear the voice disappearing as the thumping seemed to have gone downstairs.

"Don't worry about Brandon, he does this all the time, ever since his 13th birthday a few months ago. He thinks he's exceptional because he is now in the Scouts."

"Ha! Imagine him in Scouts! Brandon is always getting Elsie into trouble," said Juliana.

"One time he got me into trouble and dad had to take me to school and back, in that old patchwork automobile. It's falling apart. It's so old. It was grandmas."

"If only there was a way to stop your brother getting you into trouble all the time," said Juliana.

"Yeah, last time was terrible, especially for mum."

"Yeah, that Rottingwood gets on her nerves."

"Rotting wood?" asked Alex.

Elsie sat straight up and looked at Alex. "There's a small house at the end of our street. It's on a massive property of dead grass with old oak trees and there are always big ugly birds flying around it."

"People call it the Rottingwood," said Juliana, as she popped a flower petal into her mouth.

"I guess it has rotting wood?" asked Alex.

"Well, no one knows really, but it does look like it's made out of old, brown, mouldy, falling apart wood," replied Elsie.

Juliana looked at Alex bright-eyed and said, "And there's no front door... just an arch in the wall. People say there is a red dragon's head floating in the middle with a golden handle hanging out of its mouth and the roof is like two small wooden pyramids joined together one on top of the other."

"People from our school, The Edifin Settley School, or as we call it 'the E.S.S' say that it's been there for centuries before Humbletin was even thought of," said Elsie.

"Are you going to come to school with us, Alex?" asked Juliana. "

Umm," he didn't know what to say.

"I don't know if he can. We will have to ask Dad," said Elsie.

"You could see our lucky tree Alex. It has leaves that look like four-leaf clovers."

Alex stood up and looked out the window at The Rottingwood, thinking about his father. The expression on his face must have shown how worried he was because Elsie looked over at him and said, "Don't worry Alex we will take care of you." She sighed and continued to say, "Sometimes I feel trapped and like I don't belong here as well. Maybe one day things will change. Hopefully, Brandon will move out." Juliana laughed and flopped back on the chair, "Not likely! This weekend went so fast, if only it was longer, we could have finished our game of quoits."

"Yeah, though I think I would have won," Elsie replied.

"Elsie," said Alex, sitting back on the end of the bed, "Yes?"

"Your dad, he told me that we are inside some sort of mist."

"Yeah?"

"What's outside it?"

"Not much, really. One day I'll take you to see Josh's father. He's a scientist of astronomy and lives a few streets away."

Juliana looked at Alex and said, "You will love Josh's house. He lives in an astronomy home. Inside is a circular room with a staircase going up, up and around the inside like a giant cone shell. It feels like you're going to bash your head on the roof and then there is a big world globe at the top."

Then Elsie continued, "When you get inside the glass world globe, there is a giant telescope that's so powerful you can see through the centre of the whirlwind to the stars in the night sky. Also, you can see what is outside Humbletin."

"So, what's out there?" asked Alex.

"The scientists call it Perilisk Caveat. They say it is one of the coldest lands on the earth being covered with snow and ice, where the violent winds would chill you to the bone and ice the size of large stones fall from the sky. They say during severe lightning storms, the earth vibrates and has cracked at times, leaving deep crevasses. If you ever went out there, you would be lucky to survive from the cold. They say Humbletin only appears when Perilisk Caveat is at a certain temperature."

"I guess I'll never get out of here," replied Alex.

"Elsie did you know, Humbletin rotates around the direct centre of Perilisk Caveat," said Julie.

"Where did you hear that?"

"Josh's father was looking at some paperwork one day and I overheard him saying Humbletin is supposed to remain in the centre of Perilisk Caveat and that if it doesn't then we would all be in great peril and he looked worried."

Alex looked at Elsie and said, "I guess we are lucky to have this thick mist around us."

"Yep, without it, we would perish, and all of our nature would cease to exist."

"We would all die... All the houses would fall on us!" Juliana said, looking extremely scared with her hand over her mouth,

"It's ok Julie, nothing's going to happen."

"How do you know Elsie? We could die! What if that's what Mr Tundaweed was afraid of? We're going to die... I know we are, there are so many things I wanted to do before I died."

"Oh great, I only just get here and now I'm going to die... just perfect."

"No. no... stop it, Juliana, your scaring Alex."

"I'm not scared. I thought I was dead already anyway," laughed Alex.

"You're not dead. Stop it Julie. Its ok, nothing's going to happen. I'm sure my dad would know if something was going to happen."

"But... it could happen," replied Juliana.

"My father would know."

"He wouldn't tell us, would he?"

"Of course, he would. Dad cares about us. If something went wrong, he would want us safe. Dad always looks after us, doesn't he?"

"Well. I... I suppose your father would tell us and Josh's dad would say something, wouldn't he?"

"Yes, that's right, see..., it's ok, nothing's going to happen."

"Yeah..., I... I guess I kind of got a little carried away."

Alex looked out the window, getting lost in thought wondering how on earth he was going to get back home. His parents would be out looking for him by now. Alex suddenly had a bad feeling, what would his father... Alex remembered, 'the object must still be in my pocket.' Alex reached down to feel his pocket, 'Oh. Darn...,' he thought to himself 'I can't just pull it out here. Dad would kill me if anyone saw it.'

"Elsie?"

"Yeah?"

"Could you please show me where the bathroom is?"

"Of course," replied Elsie, as she stood up and led Alex out of the bedroom, along a hall, around a corner, past Brandon's bedroom which smelt like old smelly socks and to another door at the end of the walkway.

"Here it is."

"Thank you," replied Alex. Elsie walked back to her room.

Chapter 6. Harmonious

Alex opened the old wooden door that creaked with age. The bathroom had a high roof with a long white tube hanging down, which had a wide shower head at the end, dangling over a great round bathtub trimmed with gold that was sitting in the middle of the bathroom. A toilet with a maroon fluffy seat cover was in the corner of the room. A golden carved hand basin was against the wall opposite. Alex put his hand into his pocket and pulled out the translucent orb with tiny bubbles bouncing inside it. The bubbles were filled with different substances, some had water, dirt, fire and some hollow. He could also see cogs winding around. It started to flash again, brown, white, red, blue, Alex shook it gently. The colours stopped blinking "Oh no, I've broken it." He stood there shaking it for a while, trying to get it to work again.

In Elsie's room, Juliana was still sitting on the chair and Elsie on her bed. "Did you notice that Alex looks like Josh? Or is it just me?" asked Elsie.

"I thought he did. I was thinking it was just my eyes playing tricks on me," replied Juliana, sitting up straight on the chair. "I noticed it straight away as soon as I saw him."

"Me too, do you think he could be a relation to Josh?"

"I don't believe so. I've known Josh all my life and met most of his relatives."

"Yeah..., I think you would have recognised him if he was a relation."

"Yep."

"Hey, I got my new timetable on Friday and the new substitute teacher Miss Borrow is filling in for Mrs Glastramin in our class Creatures That Lived. Do you think the rumours are true?" Elsie sat up quickly on the side of her bed, looked at Juliana with wide eyes, a big smile and said, "I heard that she is crazy, wears a large pointy, old, floppy hat and a little nerd with glasses and big spiky hair follows her everywhere."

Juliana laughed and said, "I heard that her nails are so long that they curl, she wears a badge of a dead bird, her hair is in thousands of plaits and she has a dead vine hanging around her wrist." Elsie and Juliana laughed,

"She sounds like an old witch," said Elsie.

"Yeah, I doubt anyone could look like that... Unless they are a mad crone," laughed Juliana.

In the bathroom, Alex was getting frustrated with the object. "Why won't, this stupid thing work," he said to himself, as he shoved it back into his pocket.

"I have no idea why I'm even trying to make it work. What's the use? I can't get home and if I could, my dad would just kick me back out the door anyway."

Alex sat on the side of the bathtub with his head in his hands. 'What am I to do?' 'I can either risk my life and try to get out of this place or just give up and forget all about home.'

Alex decided to use the advice from Mr McKormick and take life one day at a time. He walked out of the bathroom and down the hallway. He couldn't stop thinking about the object and how it changed colours. CRASH! His head collided with a door that opened right in front of him, landing him on his bottom. 'Ah,' said Alex to himself, trying not to show that it hurt.

"Who are you?" said a tall chubby boy, with thick bright ginger curly hair and freckles, wearing big baggy clothes and thick glasses.

"Alex," he said standing up.

"And you are here… why? What are you doing outside my door? You were eavesdropping, weren't you? Who hired you? Did my sister put you up to this? Why are you in our house?" asked Brandon, quickly with suspicion showing on his chubby face.

"Your dad said I could stay here for a while."

"You won't be staying in my room," said the boy. He was almost like a prickly pufferfish, puffing out his chest and screwing up his face.

"Uh. Ok…," replied Alex.

The boy stomped off down the staircase and vanished out of sight.

Alex continued walking to Elsie's bedroom rubbing his head. All of a sudden just as Alex looked up, Elsie's door swung open. He jumped back making sure that this time he didn't get hit by the large wooden door. 'Phew, that was a close one,' he said to himself.

"Oh. Hi Alex," it was Juliana walking out the door.

"I have to go home now, my parents will be expecting me. Will I see you at school tomorrow?"

"I don't know, maybe."

"I'll have to ask dad," replied Elsie, standing in the doorway.

"Ok, see you in the morning."

"Yep, same time as always," replied Elsie, waving to Juliana as she walked down the stairs.

"Alex."

"Yes?"

"Do you want to come with us to school tomorrow?"

"I, well, I guess...,"

"Alright, then I can introduce you to the rest of my friends. Do you mind going down and asking dad if you can come with us tomorrow?"

"Sure, where would he be?"

"Dad should be somewhere… downstairs. Also, you might want to ask about where you are sleeping tonight."

"Good idea."

"I'll see you at dinner."

"Ok then," replied Alex, as he walked down the stairs and into the lounge room. He looked down a hallway that ran past the dining room, kitchen and to a see-through mesh back door.

Noticing one of Frank's long hairy legs with his trousers pulled up, "Is that you Mr McKormick?" he asked.

"Oh. Hi Alex," Frank popped his head around the frame of the door. "Just doing a bit of gardening before dinner. You can come on out here with me if you like," said Frank, straining as he slowly pulled a long, fat, wriggling, red worm out of the ground. It was almost the same length as Frank's long legs. He slowly placed the worm into a tall green bucket near his feet filled with more worms.

"Ewe…," replied Alex, under his breath.

"Yes, they are rather slimy. Tomorrow you could help me with the garden and do some man to man bonding if you are up to it. There's nothing better than rolling your sleeves up and getting down to earth. How does that sound?"

"Sounds. Uh… Interesting…," Alex replied, looking at the bucket of slimy worms, then to the thick bushy herbs running along the back wall of the house,

"So, did you have a nice talk with Elsie?"

"Yes, Sir. Elsie was very helpful. She explained a lot. She told me all about the scientists and how they know about what is outside Humbletin. There are strange places here, some a lot more unusual than others."

"Hmm, I think I know what you are talking about. Maybe one in particular." Frank leaned closer to Alex and whispered "The Rottingwood?"

"Yeah," Alex whispered back.

"Well. Whatever she told you, don't mention anything to Hazel."

"Mention what to me?" asked Hazel, walking out the back door carrying a basket of washing. "She has big ears this one," replied Frank laughing.

Hazel dropped the basket hard on the outside dining table and let out a 'humph...'. "Big ears hey? No dinner for you tonight, Mr Frankie," she said and walked back inside.

"Ah. She loves me," replied Frank, with a smile.

"Frank... I mean Mr McKormick."

"You can call me Frank if you like. What is it?"

"About tomorrow... Manly bonding sounds... interesting. But... Elsie and Julie...,".

"That's an excellent idea Alex. I should have thought of that myself, of course you can go with them, I'll have to discuss it with Hazel and get back in her good Books. Shouldn't be too hard. It pays to know a woman Alex. Especially what she likes." Frank gave a grin and continued, "It shouldn't be a problem. The school will be helpful for you. Just leave it with me. However, Alex, about tonight. Would you mind sleeping in the spare room? It's a bit small and cramped. You'll have to sleep on a mattress on the floor, but it would only be for tonight. Tomorrow I'll go downtown and grab a single bed for you, how does that sound?"

"You don't have to do all that for me, I may not stay that long."

"It's alright son, I mean Alex."

Alex laughed and said, "It's ok, you can call me that."

"Alrighty then." Frank had a big smile on his face. "It's no problem at all. I have already put a bag of clothing in the room for you as well. Why don't you go and get yourself settled in. I'll be in soon. Just have to wash my hands and hang out these clothes for Hazel."

"Ok," replied Alex and walked inside the back door.

To Alex's right was a blue backpack sitting in front of a door. "This must be it." He pushed on the door and SLAM! It slammed back shut "Oi you! Watch where you're going!" yelled Brandon from the other side of the door. It was the bathroom.

"Sorry." Said Alex embarrassed.

"Stay away, Stop following and spying on me! I don't want to be seen with a stray."

Alex walked further down the hallway and could see Hazel in the kitchen cooking away.

"Excuse me, Miss McCormick."

She jumped and dropped a tray of biscuits on the floor,

"Oh darn," she said, bending down to pick it up with a tea towel.

"Oh... I'm so sorry, I didn't mean to bother you, I'll go."

"No, no, it's ok, lucky I got another batch in the oven. I'm just not used to having another person in the house that's all, sorry if I frightened you, dearie."

"I'm all right."

"So, what did you want dearie?"

"I was just wondering if you could tell me where the spare room is?"

"Sure Hun. It's just around the corner, look for an arched wooden door." She pointed to her left.

"Thank you, do you want me to help...,".

"No, I'm ok for now, maybe later."

"Ok, sorry," he replied and walked around the corner to an old rickety door that was half-open.

"I guess this is it," he said to himself, as he pushed the door open, squinting his eyes as the door let out a loud deep 'Grooaan'.

In the middle of the grey carpeted room was an old patchwork bag, a white sheet, a white blanket and a white feather pillow sitting on top of a foam mattress. At the end of the bed was a heavily carved wooden chest. The other side of the bed was piled up with different items. Alex could see a small table scratching itself as if it had fleas, curtains bundled together in a corner, Boots squashed under everything, a blue lamp tipped upside- down, rolled-up posters, hats, belts, board games and lots of other bits and pieces. Alex put the sheet and blanket on the mattress and sat on it. He then pulled the object out of his pocket and put it into the bag feeling sad and untrustworthy.

He heard a familiar voice. "Mum! Mum!" yelled Elsie running down the stairs and into the kitchen CRASH!

"Ahh! Not again! Oh... Elsie! This was the last batch! There will be no cookies for you lot!"

"Awe mum I'm sorry...".

Alex felt as though he was a burden like he didn't belong anywhere. There was a knock at the door. "It's me, Elsie."

"You can come in," replied Alex. The door groaned loud as it opened, and Elsie peeked her head in. "Just thought I'd let you know dinner will be ready soon."

"Oh, ok."

"What's wrong?" asked Elsie, noticing the sad look on Alex's face.

"I... I'm ok."

"You can tell me you know, I won't tell anyone. What is it?" she asked, walking over and sitting down on the end of the mattress. Alex looked at his bag then looked at Elsie, contemplating whether to tell her about his father and the job he had been given, deciding that Elsie most probably won't believe him if he did tell her. He said, "I, I just feel like I don't fit in anywhere, with you know... This thing. Memol... Memolossity," Alex lied, feeling like he couldn't tell her the truth about the orb, not yet anyway,

"You know what?"

"What?"

"I feel like that sometimes too, feel like I am different from everyone else like I don't belong here. Like there is something out there for me that I just don't know about yet. You are not alone, Alex. Anytime you want to talk, I am here. It's not like I have a brother to talk to," laughed Elsie.

Alex nodded. "Yeah I know," he laughed.

"He didn't say anything bad or do anything to you, did he? The big bully that he is." asked Elsie.

"Nah. I just ran into his door," laughed Alex.

"Ran into his door?!" laughed Elsie.

"HaHa! Yeah! I was walking back to your room when he opened the door and I walked straight into it."

"Oh my," laughed Elsie.

"He thought that you sent me to spy on him or something."

"He is such a goofball."

"DINNERS READY!" they heard Hazel yell out.

"Come on," said Elsie, as they both stood up, walked out the door and into the dining room.

The dining room walls had old cream wallpaper with raised textured red roses. There were photos of the family all over the walls. Some photos were of a little baby pudgy Brandon, a young Hazel holding baby Elsie, young Frank standing behind her looking proud, a picture of Elsie holding up a gold trophy cup and Brandon wearing a Scouts' uniform. There was an oak table with a maroon tablecloth over it. Alex guessed maroon was Hazel's favourite colour. Around the table sat Mrs McKormick, Mr McKormick and Brandon. Alex felt like an insect being studied upon as he sat on an extra tattered chair that had been placed right at the end of the table.

"So... Alex, Frank mentioned you would like to go to school with Elsie tomorrow?" asked Hazel.

"Yes please, Mam."

"Well, I suppose it would give Elsie a chance to show you around the place."

"I agree love," replied Frank.

"Whatever," mumbled Brandon stuffing his face with food.

"Brandon……!"

"What!" replied Brandon, with a mouth full.

"You are supposed to wait until we say grace."

"Grace." replied Brandon and kept eating.

Everyone except for Brandon put their heads down and closed their eyes. Hazel began to speak, "Dear Lord, thank you for this food we are about to eat, for some people food is hard to come by and they struggle to get by every day. Please help us to help other unfortunate souls who can't find a meal, a pillow to sleep on, or clean clothes to wear. We are truly thankful for what you have given us, Amen."

Everyone said "Amen." Brandon said "Amen" with his mouth full. Alex thought about how lucky he was to have these lovely people take him in. If it weren't for them, he would have been one of the unfortunate ones Hazel had prayed about. Alex looked at Hazel and said, "Thank you for letting me stay in your home."

"Awe your welcome dear. It's such a pity other people don't give as much as they could. I'm sure if it were them on the street, it would surely change their way of thinking. There is a lot of help needed here at the moment. Everyone should be able to have a happy life while they can, especially since the…"

"Hunny...," said Frank.

"Oh, right." She started eating her dinner.

"What mum? dad?" asked Elsie.

"Don't worry Elsie, nothing to be concerned about," replied Frank. Alex couldn't stop thinking about his parents and the orb in his bag. 'I wonder what it is and how it works' he thought to himself. Brandon stopped eating and looked like something was running through his mind. Alex could almost see his brain mechanism straining to work.

"Mum I'll be going to Bryan's on Friday for the weekend."

"That's good to hear love," replied Hazel, while waving her hands at the dishes on the table, instructing them to go to the sink, Alex watched them fly past, one almost hitting him in the face.

After dinner Alex sat on the front step of the house and looked at the beautiful stars and clouds on the road, thinking how many people would love to be able to see what he saw right now. The front door creaked as it opened a tiny bit. Alex looked down beside him as he felt something touch his leg. There was a slender tonkinese cat. A bell with a star and moon hung off a collar with diamonds that was around its neck. His fur was light brown. His feet were white and on his top lip were two white stripes like vampire's teeth. The cat sat next to him and rubbed its head against Alex's hand. "You want a pat, do you?" The cat looked at him as to say, 'Yes of course I do. Why else would I be sitting here for?' Alex smiled and stroked the cat's fur from his nose to the tip of the cat's tail. His coat glistened in the moonlight.

"His name is Pussin Boo," said Elsie, standing at the front door.

"Oh sorry, I didn't realise you were standing there."

"It's alright, I'm surprised he has let you near him. Pussin Boo is very picky with whom he will befriend. Do you mind if I joined you?"

"I don't mind."

Elsie sat down next to Pussin Boo and scratched under his neck. "So how do you like it here so far?"

"You know, I'm actually starting to like it. Your parents have been so kind to me."

Alex stared at the sky thinking about what his parents would be doing at this moment then said, "So why did you call him Pussin Boo?"

"Well, it all started five years ago, back when Pussin Boo's name was Pussin Boots. On Halloween night, my friends and I were playing hide-n-seek and Pussin Boots was wondering around the lounge room. Sally, one of my old school friends, was playing seeker. She jumped around the corner and there was Boots. He was that scared his fur was sticking up in the air. He ran straight into where I was, climbed up onto me with his claws and would not let me go.

He was hissing at everything that went anywhere near him. It took me a whole week to calm him down again since that night Boo has been scared of everything and now his name is Pussin Boo or Boo for short."

"Ha, He seems alright now."

"Yes, you must be one of the lucky ones."

All went silent as they watched the clouds drift past. The full moon was shining brightly.

Then a head poked out the door.

"Elsie's got a boyfriend. Elsie's got a boyfriend."

"Shut Up, Brandon! I'm going to kill you!" screamed Elsie running inside after him with Boo running after her, Alex laughed as he stood up and walked inside, making sure the door was locked.

When Alex went into his room, Hazel was fluffing up his soft feather down pillow.

"Why don't you go ahead and put your things inside the chest at the end of your bed, dear."

"Are you sure it's ok that I use this Mrs McKormick?"

"Of cause, you can love, just try not to damage it too much. It was my grandmothers. Make sure you get dressed into your pyjamas sweet, then off to bed. I will see you in the morning ready for school." She kissed his forehead and walked off, up the stairs. Alex carefully opened the chest. A beautiful smell of fresh cedar wood came wafting out. He opened the old bag that Mr McKormick had given him, pulled out the orb and put it at the bottom of the chest. He then pulled out some clothes that looked like they were Mr McKormick's and put them over the top of the orb. He dressed in his pyjamas, turned off the light and laid on his bed. Elsie peeked through a gap in the door "Goodnight Alex."

"Night."

Chapter 7. School

The next morning, Alex awoke feeling refreshed and renewed. While getting dressed, he thought about the unusual dream he had last night with strange creatures he had never seen before. There were lizards with aqua eyes and coloured spikes on their backs and baby dragons in every colour you could think of. The flame that came from their mouth was bright blue and harmless. There were tiny fluffy kittens. Some had rainbow-coloured fur.

There was a knock on the door. "Come in!" said Alex, sitting on his mattress. The door swung open and Else was standing there. "Mum said to come and get you for breakfast." She looked at Alex and screwed up her face "You're not wearing that are you?" Alex was wearing a pair of old grey knee-length pants, a green and yellow shirt and a pair of old brown leather Boots.

"Uhhm…," said Alex, as he looked down at himself.

"Come with me," said Elsie, as she gestured for him to follow. They walked up the stairs and to Elsie's room.

"Here take these." She walked over to the dresser and pulled out a red and black striped short-sleeved school shirt with a collar and a black tie.

"You're lucky I have a spare sports shirt. I don't have any shorts for you, although you might look good in one of my skirts," she giggled.

Alex laughed. "No, it's ok."

Elsie gave Alex the shirt and tie. "Ok, put them on" Alex looked at her then started to unbutton his shirt,

"No, no, not in here" she giggled and pointed out the door. "In the bathroom."

"Oh, right," said Alex, going a shade of red. He went to the bathroom, put them on and came back. "Better?"

"Much better, but those Boots are awful." Elsie grabbed a pair of her black sports shoes and a pair of socks and handed them to Alex. "Put these on too." He sat on the chair and put them on.

Elsie sat on her bed and put on her black laced shoes with white knee-length socks.

Alex stood up, put his arms out and said, "Tada! How do I look?"

Elsie laughed "Yes, that's much better, I could just imagine you wearing one of my pleated black skirts."

"Ha-ha, no thanks," chuckled Alex.

Elsie laughed, "Ok, let's go down for breakfast".

When they went down to the dining room, Mr McKormick was sitting at the table happily reading the newspaper and Mrs McKormick was boiling a pot of tea in the fireplace. Brandon was slumping over the table with jam all over his face, a piece of toast in one of his hands and a thick Book in the other. On the front cover it said, Scouts 101. He was dressed in his brown and green Scouts uniform. Elsie sat down and Alex sat in his chair at the end of the table next to Brandon. "What, what!" yelled Brandon.

Alex leaned away from Brandon like he was about to get his head bitten off. Brandon looked up at Alex. "Oh, it's just you," then kept eating and reading. Alex buttered himself a piece of toast.

"Morning, Mum, Dad…… Brandon…, did anyone hear anything last night?"

"What do you mean sweetie?" asked her mother.

"I thought I heard people talking last night."

"I didn't hear anything my sweet. The only thing I heard was your father's snoring, took me forever to fall asleep." Her mother gave her father a nasty look. Mr McKormick gave a big grin.

"Oh, ok," Elsie replied, then squeezed some blueberry syrup onto her pancakes.

"The spooks from the Rottingwood have come to get you, Elsie, they want to tell you something," Brandon said, staring at Elsie with bulging eyes like they were going to pop out. "WooOOoo…," he said, trying to be scary. He pushed out his fat lips looking like a fish and waving his arms around like an octopus. Then he stuffed his face with jammed toast, dropping bits onto his Book, which he gladly licked off of the paper.

"Very funny Brandon… I'm going to be attacked by a fish with octopus' arms, am I? Cause that is what you look like" He looked up and her and said, "Well, I'll tell you what you look like…".

"Brandon!" bellowed Frank looking at him.

"What dad… she started it…". He looked at his mum "Mum…".

"Don't get me involved," she replied.

Brandon screwed up his face and shoved toast in his mouth whilst giving Elsie evil looks.

"So, are you looking forward to your first day at school, Alex? I see you found a uniform, looks good on you," said Mr McKormick.

"Uhh... Thanks. Yeah, can't wait," he replied, looking a little worried considering what he has seen of Humbletin so far.

"It's ok, nothing to be worried about. I'm sure you will have so much fun. The time will fly, and you will be back home in no time at all."

Alex sighed when he heard the word 'home.' All he could think about was his family and if they were missing him right now. He wondered what his dad would be thinking. Would he be mad that he didn't come home, or would he believe Alex was still travelling?

"Ready Alex?" asked Elsie, as she grabbed her red and black school bag and wide brim hat off the round glass fishbowl table in the lounge room.

"Sure...," he replied, standing up and picking up his plates to take to the kitchen.

"Don't worry about these. I will take care of them, Alex. Just have a great day and don't forget to eat your lunch. I have put it in your bag over near Elsie's," said Hazel, as she pointed to the patchwork bag on the fishbowl table. Alex walked over and picked up his bag. They said their goodbyes as they walked outside where Juliana was waiting.

"Morning Elsie, Alex. We'd better hurry to school, or we might be late".

Walking down the path, Elsie said "Sorry I'm late. I wanted to give Alex some school stuff."

"Looks good," replied Juliana.

"Thank you." Alex looked at Juliana, then Elsie and smiled. Elsie blushed,

"So, Alex, what did you think of Brandon?" asked Juliana.

They walked past a large tree that was bent over. It was making a soft humming noise like a lullaby, while one of its branches were touching a smaller tree.

"I don't know how Elsie puts up with him."

"Neither do I," replied Juliana.

"I wish I didn't have to, but for now, I do, so I just ignore him." A screeching, high pitched woman's voice shrieked out "Get away! Get away! You! You! And you! get away!"

"Minx! run!" yelled Juliana as they all ran down the road then stopped, as they got far enough away that they could no longer hear the screeching.

"What was that all about?" asked Alex.

"See the tiny houses that we ran past." Juliana turned around and pointed back to row upon row of tiny olive green, houses. "Yeah," he replied, feeling out of breath.

"Tiny Elfish folk live there. Most of them are happy go lucky little people, but not Grandmamma Minx. They call her that because she has a pet minx that curls up around her shoulders. She screams at you like you just heard then if you go anywhere near her purple plumatoes. She carries around a grass garden broom to shoo people away. Sometimes she puts a curse on them. Normally we would go around her place. Everyone tends to avoid her".

"No wonder why," replied Alex, putting his finger in his ears wiggling them. Elsie pointed to extensive gardens next to the other houses. "The Elfish gardens are magic. That's where I get my flowers from. They are so precious to them, so they spend most of their lives working in their gardens, protecting them."

"Magic gardens?" asked Alex.

"They use a special green growing spell that makes their cabbages, plumatoes, flowers and herbs grow to gigantic proportions, bigger than the Elfish themselves."

"Wow look at that flower," said Alex, pointing to a house with huge flowers hanging over it.

"Oh... That's Samuel. He has at least half a dozen giant umbreleanas surrounding his garden. The one shading his house is the largest," said Juliana.

They started walking again, Elsie looked at Juliana. "You know Samuel?"

"Well. I don't know Samuel personally, but he visits us on the odd occasion to see father about something."

"I get my flowers off Samuel," replied Elsie.

Down the pathway, they could see a figure of a boy waiting at the school gate.

"Josh!" yelled Juliana running towards him giving him a big hug. Elsie and Alex slowly walked up to them.

"Josh meet Alex. He is staying at my house for a while," said Elsie.

 "Nice to meet you," said Josh.

"You too," Alex replied.

"Zhè shì shuí??!?"

Juliana looked behind her and said, "Oh... Hi Lilly. Alex, this is Lilly. She is another one of our good friends."

"Hi, Lilly."

"Hi."

Lilly had tawny skin. Her eyes single lidded, wide-set and her hair was straight, black, long and looked like silk.

"Lilly's father says their ancestors come from a place called China," said Elsie. "But no one has ever heard of such a place," said Josh. "Hey!" said Lilly embarrassed.

"Sorry Lilly," said Josh.

"Lilly's very touchy on that subject," Elsie whispered to Alex. Lilly glared at Elsie.

"But Lilly's father says they are from a rare ancient culture and that he has proof and no matter if it's true or not, it doesn't matter. Friends are friends no matter where they come from." She smiled at Lilly. Lilly smiled back.

Alex spoke up and said, "That's right Elsie. Some people don't believe me when I say I don't come from Humbletin, but it's true and Lilly, I do believe you. I have seen China on TV when I was home in Ireland."

Lilly looked at Alex with tears in her eyes. "I know I am different... but you don't have to make up stuff." She turned around and started walking off mumbling under her breath 'TV...., Ireland..., what stupid made-up names."

"I guess no one believes me. I'm sorry. I didn't mean to upset Lilly. I was trying to say, I know how she feels."

"It's ok Alex. Lilly is very touchy when anyone talks about her culture," replied Elsie.

"You know, she even yelled at my mum once," chuckled Josh.

"It's not funny," said Juliana.

"It was when Lilly called her an old know it all bag. You should have seen my mum's face".

Elsie tried not to laugh. "Your mother was never one to be put in her place. I can imagine her screwed up face, like an old, shrivelled prune." She burst out with laughter. Juliana giggled.

Alex seemed confused. He couldn't figure out why they were saying nasty things about Josh's mother. "Don't you like your mum?"

 Josh said "Honestly, I don't know my mum much. We have never really connected. She is always over my brother's house. John is 33, owns a block of land and mum goes there a lot. I don't really know John much either. He spent most of his life away from home."

Elsie looked into the front schoolyard. "Come on. Let's go show Alex our lucky tree." Elsie and her friends walked into the schoolyard and over to the tree.

"Why don't you go with your mum to your brother's?" asked Alex, walking next to Josh.

"I have thought about it, but it's more complicated than that".

Chapter 8. Resolution

A loud scream echoed through the schoolyard. They looked for where it was coming from and under a tree outside of the school was Brandon, all scrunched up wriggling his fingers and screaming frantically.

"Ahh, get it off, get it off." There was something big, black, brown and furry on his head. Brandon must have been following Elsie to school. Elsie gave her bag to Juliana and walked over to Brandon. She looked angry,

"What are you doing here, boofhead? Are you following me again???" asked Elsie.

"Get it off, you little rat! Just get it off," replied Brandon.

"Why should I? You followed me here and... You just called me a rat!" "I didn't mean to, just get it off!"

"Only if you promise me...,"

"What! What! Promise what? I do not promise you anything!" said Brandon quickly, shaking scared still wriggling his fingers. "Fine, I'll just leave you to it then. Bye," said Elsie. She turned and started to walk away.

Elsie glanced at her friends. Lilly had come back to sit under the tree. They were all talking to each other casually as if Brandon's behaviour was a usual routine. Alex was still talking about Josh and his family.

Elsie sighed in relief.

"Wait, wait, ok, I will," said Brandon.

"I thought as much," Elsie said, turning back around and walking up to Brandon.

"What, what do you want," said Brandon, now looking like a frozen popsicle.

Elsie looked into his big square thick glasses and whispered at him, "Stop following me. It's my life, not yours."

"No way, you can't make me!" replied Brandon forcefully, but trying not to move.

"Ok, I will go now, shall I?" said Elsie.

"No, no, don't go," he moved. Something long, thin and furry fell down the front of his face.

Another loud scream came from Brandon. Elsie cupped her ears with her hands.

"Get it off, just get it off. I will! I will leave you alone!"

"Promise! Promise on Grandma's grave!" said Elsie. Now staring deep into his eyes, with a look of wonder.

The question 'will he say it' was running through her mind.

Brandon looked back at Elsie with fear. He knew Grandma McKormick loved Elsie, and whenever Brandon stepped out of line, he would pay for it. Brandon had a flashback of getting his mouth washed out with soap and plucking out ten long hairs under Grandma's chin, once a week, for six weeks, as one of his punishments.

"I, I, promi... Oh...... Do I have to?"

"Unless you want me to walk away? You know I can if I want to."

"On, Gra, Gran, Grandma's grave!" said Brandon. Now with his eyes closed, scrunched up into a ball. "Now get it ooooffff!" Elsie quickly grabbed the thing off his head. "And if you don't keep your promise, I will tell everyone about what just happened. Look!" said Elsie. Brandon opened his eyes and looked at a big, wrinkly, furry, black and brown... leaf in her hands.

"You, you tricked me! You little rat! YOU TRICKED ME!" yelled Brandon.

"Yep, I sure did," replied Elsie, with a smirk. Brandon gave Elsie a scrunched-up frown.

"You better keep your promise," said Elsie, holding out the leaf.

"I, I will get you back for this one-day Elsie and, and that's a promise!" said Brandon and stomped off down the road. Elsie walked back to the lucky tree. all her friends were now looking at her clapping and cheering her on. Elsie had a smile from ear to ear.

An eerie, high pitch, pristine whistle of a pleasant melody, echoed gently, flowing through the school grounds, as the school phoenix sang for classes to begin.

Elsie, Juliana, Lilly, Josh and Alex strolled off to art class. They walked inside a big white room.

"What is that?" asked Alex, looking at a giant machine that looked like it was made out of solid white bubbles all joined together.

"An orb projector," replied Lilly.

A mass of students walked through the door, just about knocking them over.

"This here, is an orb projector," announced a man walking into the room, holding a staff made out of twisted wood, with a giant golden orb on top. He had shoulder-length curly black hair. He was wearing long black jeans, a white button-up shirt and big black Boots.

"We will be using this orb projector today to make an orb film. Forgive me, we have a new student here today. For all who does not remember my name, I am Mr Bucklesworth, and this here is your new classmate, Alex. The man pointed to Alex. So where are you from Alex?"

"I'm from Irela... Humbletin."

Mr Bucklesworth laughed. "Of course, you are boy, ok now that was are all introduced, we will begin".

Elsie turned and whispered into Alex's ear, "Lilly has a crush on Mr Bucklesworth. She tells me all the time." She tried to imitate Lilly's voice, still whispering in his ear. "He has a unique physique. His ringlets are to die for, so wonderfully striking, yet his diminutive whiskers under his nose makes him look so handsome." Elsie giggled. Alex laughed. Josh stared at Alex. He was usually the one getting Elsie's attention.

"Excuse me, Elsie, is there something funny you would like to share with the class?"

"No Sir, I mean, Mr Bucklesworth," replied Elsie.

"Well, come on class, what are you waiting for? Hasten your pace an, get those orbs up there!"

Orbs flew out of the orb projector and into the middle of the room. They looked almost like tiny bubbles. The classroom was filled with loud voices coming from each student trying to command the orbs. Getting muddled up and confused the orbs were bumping into each other and bouncing off of the walls.

"Now I know why the room has nothing in it!" exclaimed Alex.

Mr Bucklesworth was standing with the students, looking up at the orbs saying, "Get up there, you scallywags," "Go on orb," "Next to ya matey." He then began to whistle a tune. One of the orbs started sounding like a bell, then another sound like a harp, another a violin, another a thumping sound. One by one, they swept through the room in harmony, making a rhythm. There were thousands of orbs flying everywhere, weaving in, out and around each other. The class began to whistle with him. Mr Bucklesworth was as thrilled as could be. All of the orbs were coming together perfectly.

"Good going young broods." He cleared his throat. "I mean students, you all deserve a pat on the back." Lilly blushed and giggled.

Floating in the air were orbs, shaped together forming an old moving pirate ship, sailing on the ocean. The pirates on the ship were fighting off a giant sea troll, everyone clapped and cheered. When the class had finished, Alex walked out to the school gate with his new friends. "That was a great lesson," said Alex. "Yes, it was," replied Lilly, still flustered.

"That tune he was whistling…, I've heard it before."

"It's one of his favourite songs," replied Lilly dreamily.

"I'm sure I heard it in a stage performance. It was about, Pirates, called…. Pirate chest… no, Pirate Gol… No, I can't remember."

"The Rottingwood!" yelled Josh.

"Uh... No... I don't think that was it," replied Alex.

Everyone stopped what they were doing and looked at him. "What are you talking about Josh?" asked Juliana, looking at him curiously.

"Ok... I know you all might think I am crazy for suggesting this but... Halloween is coming up and I've been thinking that we should do something. Like... maybe... going to The Rottingwood and Yes! I have given it some thought. We have all suffered enough already, haven't we? Our parents begging us not to go there. Hearing about it day in and day out. We can't step outside the front door without someone telling us not to go to that end of the street. Some of us have even hidden behind trees to escape our parents following us to school because they don't trust us! All I'm trying to say is... I think we should put an end to all this mystery stuff and find out for ourselves what it really is. I mean it could just be an empty building for all we know, and I don't know about any of you. However, I've spent all my life dreaming about that place and wondering what on earth is in it. Tell me who here has not wondered what was over there?" They all looked down at their feet thinking about the past events. Josh was pacing up and down the pathway, in front of the school gate. You could see the frustration within him.

Josh stopped in front of them and said "If we at least checked it out, it could put an end to all this rubbish, even if it was just for ourselves so that we didn't dream about it, night, after night. Some of us might get caught, maybe even punished by our parents, but just think about the outcome. No more dreams, no more wondering, no more staring out your window at it, without that name haunting us in our minds, our nightmares, our thoughts. Besides what could they do to us if we get caught? It can't be anywhere near the things we have suffered from that place. I have decided I am going. If anyone wants to join me you can, but I have made up my mind."

"I will," said Lilly.

"Just wait a minute. I think we should have time to think about this," said Juliana.

"What's to think about?" asked Lilly.

"It sounds dangerous to me," said Alex, as he bent down and tied his shoelace.

"Elsie, what do you think?" asked Juliana, looking at her.

"I," she sighed, took in a big gulp of air and continued. "I'm sick and tired of mum going on and on about that place. I want to at least know what exactly she is going on about. I know she will kill me if she finds out, but I can't keep living with this, this Rottingwood place is like a flea on me that I can't get off! Actually, it almost sounds like my brother."

"Well then, I guess we go," replied Juliana.

"Then that's, that." Josh picked up his bag off the ground and walked out the school gate with Lilly. "Bye, see you tomorrow." They waved goodbye to Josh and Lilly.

"Elsie, this sounds very dangerous to me. I don't think we should go, if you get into trouble or hurt," said Alex, as he turned to face Elsie and Juliana.

"I know," replied Elsie, thinking that she couldn't believe she had agreed. "Well, we can't back out now and, in a way, I really do want to know what the big deal is. However, we have to be careful. My brother is a Pratt and loves to get me into trouble. Also, he now wants to get back at me for this morning. I did manage to get him to promise me he would stay away, but if I get caught, I will have to bath our portlyfouls for a year!"

"What's portlyfouls?" asked Alex.

"You know what a sheep is?"

"Yeah"

"Well, Portlyfouls are like sheep, except two times fatter, lumpy, have long straight black, white or grey hair and have a flat face with a round pink nose. The hair is extremely smelly, like old socks."

"They smell like your brother's room then?" laughed Alex.

"Ha-ha, yeah I guess they do. Portlyfouls need to be washed, brushed, then their hair cut for knitting or selling and if I get caught that's exactly what I'll be doing for a whole year. Mum would be so angry with me. She would probably get me to do the dishes for a year as well!" distressed Elsie.

"Don't worry. I will make sure that Brandon doesn't see you and if he does, I will say it's my fault. I asked you to show me around Humbletin. Everything will be ok," said Alex, putting his hand on Elsie's back for support. Juliana picked up her bag. "I'm sorry, but I've got to run. My step mum is taking me out shopping." Juliana looked at Elsie, expressing sympathy, then waved goodbye as she walked out the gate.

Alex looked up at the sun as it was going down behind a group of trees in the distance. "We better go before your brother decides to come get us." They picked up their bags and headed off down the road.

Chapter 9. To Ponder

Walking down the road, Elsie noticed there was no noise. The street was empty. All the lights were on in the houses. They were alone.

"So…., your father tells me he is trying to fix the sodcurtail mower in your front yard," said Alex, saying anything that came into his head. Elsie was watching a blue arched lamp post shaking flies away from its light as they were getting closer to it.

"Oh, that old stubborn thing. Father has tried to fix it millions of times, but it just doesn't want to be fixed, he has tried everything".

"Didn't Josh say that he fixes things? Why don't you ask him?"

"Oh… I don't know…," replied Elsie, with her head down.

"What's wrong?" asked Alex.

Elsie looked up at him and continued with a sigh. "Well. Josh used to be so much fun, but then all of a sudden…"

"He changed?"

"Yeah… When he got into this business with his dad."

"You mean… Uhh, what did he say? T… U… S.., no, T… R…,"

"T... R... U... M... S. 'The Rebuilding Unfinished Miscellany Society'. He has been like this for a couple of months, makes me wonder...,"

"If he will stay that way?"

"Yeah...,"

"I know how you feel. My father has changed. We used to have so much fun when I was little."

"Sorry, Alex. I don't mean to load my frustrations onto you."

"It's ok. It's not like I'm going to tell anyone is it?"

"That's true. You know, I do feel sorry for Josh."

"Why is that?"

"He is so proud of his father's work, but the kids at school tease him all the time. They say that he was adopted and that he is a nobody and that his father's business is in shambles."

"Poor guy. Why do they say he was adopted?"

Elsie didn't say a word. I doubt she even heard Alex. She was no longer by his side. Alex turned around and saw Elsie further back staring across the road at a red-flowered bush.

"Elsie? What is it? Is there something in the bush?" Alex squinted his eyes, trying to see what it was.

"No......,"

"Then what?"

"It's…. It's…,"

"It's what?"

"I… I don't know."

"Let me have a look," replied Alex, walking across the road to what Elsie was looking at.

"Ok… Well… I'll… I'll just wait here then."

"Alright."

"Alex, Alex!" Elsie called out.

He looked back, "Yes?"

"Be… Be careful, over there."

"Ok!"

Alex ambled up to the bush, taking a closer look at what seemed to be a blue wooden box. 'Scratch, scratch.' He stepped back the scratching was getting louder. He thought to himself 'don't move to fast, it could be dangerous'. He carefully walked closer to the box, noticing there was no lid. He gently shifted the branches, when suddenly 'whoosh' something flew out of the box. Alex jumped backwards.

"Alex! are you ok?" yelled Elsie.

"I'm fine," he said, moving the rest of the branches out of the way. Alex froze still staring into the box. He pinched himself. 'Ouch.' There was a tiny, fury, rainbow-coloured kitten, looking up at him with bright blue eyes. It opened its mouth.

What came out you would not believe. The kitten started to talk.

"Don't be scared, Alex." Its voice was like an aerie high pitch whisper. Alex turned around to see if Elsie was still there.

"What are you doing? What is it?" yelled Elsie from across the street. Alex turned back to the box and the kitten was gone. He stood there for a while not knowing what to do. What to think or what to say. Was it another dream? Did he just experience an illusion or just going completely insane?

"Are you ok?" asked Elsie, now standing behind him. He jumped "Ah.. I... you scared me."

"You've been standing over here for quite some time. I was starting to worry about you."

"I'm ok," he replied.

"What were you doing?"

"I was... Just..." Alex looked around at the tree and saw a tiny bug sitting under it. "I was just looking at this bug. I've never seen one like this before. I wonder what it is called." He reached down to pick it up.

"No, don't do that."

"Why not?"

"Because it could be poisonous."

"It doesn't look it and it's kind of cute,"

Elsie had a closer look at it. "Awe it is, isn't it." the bug was black with red dots and big eyes.

"It's smaller than my little fingernail. What could it possibly do to me?" He bent over to pick it up, but a lizard ran in front of his hand. Elsie let out a scream as a loud sucking, slurping noise came from the bug. Then as fast as you could say bogey, the bug opened it's sharp-toothed mouth and gobbled up the lizard whole. The bug no longer looked like a little bug. It was now looking more like a huge ugly slug slithering under the bush until they could no longer see it. "What Was That?" asked Alex, shocked.

"I... oh... My... I don't know, that was just... weird."

"Let's get out of here before anything else happens," replied Alex, still in shock. They walked back onto the path looking extremely confused.

"So... So.... do you like plants and stuff... like your dad does?" asked Alex, trying to change the subject.

"I do, like plants and herbs. It's amazing some of the things you can use them for."

"I know a bit about plants. My mother is a gardener."

"You remember your mother?"

Alex sighed, "I wish people would believe me. I do remember... honestly...,"

"Sorry Alex, I wish I could tell you what you want to hear."

"It's ok. So, have you ever seen a plant called the Venus Flytrap?" asked Alex, changing the subject again.

"I don't think so."

"It's a plant that swallows flies. It dissolves them in its belly."

"Ewe." Elsie screwed up her face, laughed and said, "We have a fruit out the back called a Gramatoe. It has dark purple berries that taste like grapes and tomatoes."

"That would taste weird," replied Alex, as they approached the house.

"MUM! DAD! Elsie and Alex are home!" They could see Brandon peeking through a gap in the front door, then his little chubby head popped back into the house.

"Mum, why does that boy have to be here." They could hear his voice whispering behind the front door.

"Because he is our guest."

"I don't like him."

Elsie looked at Alex and giggled.

"Quiet, I have to let them in," said Mrs McKormick.

"No, no, don't let them in. Can't he stay somewhere else?"

"Why?"

"Because."

"Don't be silly now move out of the way." 'CREAK…' the door opened slowly. They could see Brandon glaring at them, standing next to Mrs McKormick. "Come in. It must be cold out there."

"Thanks, mum," replied Elsie.

Mrs McKormick moved aside to let them in. Brandon was giving Elsie the death stare as they walked past.

"Alex! Just the man I need. Come out the back, son! I have something to show you!" Frank was standing at the back door, waving to Alex for him to come outside.

Elsie walked into the kitchen to get a drink of watermelon freshy. She sat on a tall spinning stool at a circular table in the middle of the kitchen, thinking about the walk home, watching the folks and spoons dancing together on the table. Wooden spoons started tapping on the back of bowls, as the forks and spoons danced to the beat. Butter knives were walking around studying jar labels on the shelves. Teacups were in the kitchen sink spinning on top of the water, swishing around to the music. A soup spoon started singing to Elsie, "It's not unusual to be loved by anyone," in a deep voice. Elsie giggled.

A transparent multi-coloured tablecloth was spinning around reshaping itself in the air making beautiful patterns. Little drink umbrellas were spinning, floating up, then down. Elsie stood up and started to dance to the music happily.

A loud annoying croaky voice cut across the spoons singing to the tune, "Elsie's got a boyfriend, ha-ha…, Elsie and Alex…, kissy…, kissy-kissy…," The music stopped. Everything went still. Elsie looked at Brandon and went bright red with anger and embarrassment. She shouted out loud, "Shut up, Brandon! Go pick on someone your own size!".

"Elsie is calling me fat again mum!"

Hazel yelled out from another room, "Elsie! Don't pick on your brother! You know he is big boned!" Brandon looked at Elsie with his great big screwed up grin, then promptly began poking fun at Elsie again, singing and waving his arms around, pretending to be Elsie and Alex kissing and waltzing together. Elsie walked over to Brandon.

Brandon cowered and put his face over his head thinking that Elsie was going to hit him.

"You will regret this you, you, you ugly toad," she retorted then stormed off upstairs.

Mr McKormick walked inside quickly, saw Brandon doing the dance and grabbed Brandon's ear.

"Hazel! Come see your boy!" Mrs McKormick came running down the stairs. Alex peeked in the back door.

"What happened? What happened?" she asked.

"Your son was doing a stupid dance, imitating his sister," he said, letting go of Brandon's ear.

"What!?! Brandon! How dare you! It's enough with you asking me not to let your sister in the house! This is the last straw." Mrs McKormick grabbed his ear and led him upstairs to the bathroom with Mr McKormick following.

Alex could hear Brandon yelling out "NO! NO! not the soap! NO!"

"You are getting that filthy mouth of yours washed out with soap! NOW STAY STILL!" yelled Hazel.

Alex laughed and sat at a wooden dining table in the back yard, which was lit with floating orbs. Thinking about all of the things that happened that day at school and on the way home, Alex was very confused about the way he had been feeling. 'This place is so weird, things moving..., everything alive, the people are different. However, it just feels... So...,' He thought with a broad smile on his face. "So... nice," Alex said out loud and looked up at the floating orbs in the air and thought about the object his Father had given him, that was in his room right now.

"I think I'll go and have another look," he said to himself, stood up and went to walk inside when Hazel noticed him as she came down the stairs. "Alex!" yelled Mrs McKormick.

"Yes Mam?"

"Could you help me set up the table out the back, love?"

"Sure." She handed him a lavender coloured tablecloth.

"Lay this over the table and tell it not to move or else...,"

"Or else?"

"It's a hypnotic word so that it stays still."

"Ok... Sure...,"

Alex walked outside struggling with the cloth as it began to wriggle, squirming around trying to escape the firm grip. He laid the fabric onto the table.

"Stay still."

The cloth wriggled on the table. "Stay, stay still or...,"

It flattened itself onto the table moving a little and shivering. "Or else." The cloth flopped and didn't move at all. "Hm, that's better," said Alex, walking back inside for more to put on the table,

"Here, Elsie," said Mrs McKormick. Elsie had her pj's on helping her mother in the kitchen. "Take these out to the table with Alex, then sit down." She handed them some large bowls with pasta, rice, mince, potatoes and vegetables,

"Yes mum."

"Yes, Mam."

"You know, Alex... you could call me mum if you like. Elsie's other friends call me mum."

"Uhh... Ok... mum," said Alex, smiling feeling a little embarrassed. After setting out the table, Alex and Elsie sat across from each other.

"Don't worry about it. She is used to a lot of people calling her mum. Even dad sometimes calls her mum," she giggled.

Alex looked away with a smile on his face blushing. He wasn't used to being around girls.

Chapter 10. The Way Is Clear.

The school phoenix squawked it was time to go to class. You could see everyone in the schoolyard heading off to their lessens or getting their things ready.

"Darn... I forgot my timesheet. Elsie do you know what class we have?" asked Juliana.

"Sure, I have my timesheet right here... Our Teacher is.... Miss Borrow...," said Elsie, in a disappointed voice.

"Oh man...,"

"Who's Miss Borrow?" asked Alex.

"You don't want to know," said Josh.

"You'll see," replied Juliana, putting her bag onto her back.

"Let's go and get it over and done with," said Lilly.

Juliana, Elsie, Josh, Lilly and Alex walked out from under the tree, over a green hill and down into the classroom corridor when suddenly...

"What is that smell?" asked Alex.

"I don't know, but I think it is coming from our class," replied Elsie.

"And what is that?" Alex was looking down beside the classroom door. There were two pumpkins, with a face carved into them. Inside was a candle that smelt like roses and strawberries. They all walked into class.

The smell of sandalwood wafted through the room. Bats were flying around the ceiling.

Desks were carved in pictures of pumpkin heads and cobwebs were hanging in each corner of the room with realistic spiders crawling around. Alex got shivers going down his spine, thinking about the spiders at Stonehenge.

Elsie and Juliana looked at each other and said, "Halloween."

"I forgot it was today!"

"So did I!"

"Rottingwood," Elsie whispered under her breath. Juliana looked worried.

Miss Borrow had grey, long wavy hair and was wearing a long old dress that looked like it had been hanging in a wardrobe for over 100 years. A badge of a phoenix was pinned close to her shoulder.

Alex looked at Miss Borrow who was glaring at them in distaste. "Elsie, Josh and the rest of you sit down. You are late. You know what your punishment is for being late, don't you?

Anyone who turns up late in my class has to clean the classroom after the class has finished."

"Clean the classroom," said a squeaky voice, that came from a tiny thin boy with light, ginger curly hair, lots of freckles and was wearing glasses. He stood at about 3'5 next to Miss Borrow.

Miss Borrow suddenly smiled and said, "But not today! So, think yourselves lucky. Today is Halloween and nobody gets punishments."

"No one," repeated the boy.

"Welcome Everyone to Mythology. Now everyone get out your Books. Today, we will be studying Runes and Mythological Symbols."

"Wow that class was great!" said Alex, throwing down his backpack and sitting under the lucky tree.

"I know. She wasn't anything like what people have been saying," replied Elsie, sitting down next to him.

"So, is everyone ready for tonight?" asked Josh.

"I... I can't go," said Lilly, standing up grabbing her bag and walking off with her head low.

"Well then, I guess it's just us four? We will meet out front of Elsie's at five-thirty. Sound good?" said Josh. Everyone nodded and went on their way home.

"Mum. We are going now," yelled Elsie as she walked outside the front of her house with Alex following behind.

"Wait pumpkin, you can't go yet." She could hear her mum yelling out and could see her running to the door looking like she was having a stress attack. "Pumpkin, you can't go without this."

"Oh, but why mum? Do I have to," said Elsie, sounding very miserable.

"Yes darling. You should know it's bad luck to go without it on Halloween." Mrs McKormick put a ring of platted cat hair over Elsie's head and around her neck, looking at her with a big smile and said, "See darling. It's not that bad is it. Now go and have a great time with your friends."

"Thanks, mum," said Elsie, as her mum gave her a big kiss on the cheek then walked inside.

Elsie stood there for a moment thinking about how much her mother loved her. A giggle came from behind a big tree. Elsie walked out into the front yard. "Come on, come out I know you are there," said Elsie out loud.

Juliana jumped out from behind one of the trees. "Boo! So, your mum made you wear that again?"

Josh stepped out from behind another.

"Yeah, but I don't mind really." Replied Elsie.

"So, any plans on how we are getting to the Rottingwood place," asked Alex, pointing to the end of the street. Elsie grabbed his hand and whispered, "Shh… remember we are not supposed to be going there. My parents might hear you and they could be watching us right now" Elsie looked around at the house windows, couldn't see anyone and then back at Alex. She wondered why he wasn't saying anything just staring at her. Elsie then realised how blue Alex's eyes were. Then she looked down, noticing that she was still holding onto his hand. Elsie blushed as she let go.

"Uh, I, I suppose we need to figure that out," she replied.

"Well, my Dad has gone out for the night and I have the key to get into the house."

"Good idea, Julie," replied Josh, moving closer to Elsie and looking at Alex with uncertainty.

On the way to Juliana's house, Alex walked behind everyone, having a good look around the streets and houses. He suddenly noticed a boy who looked a lot like Brandon heading through someone's yard behind them. The boy looked as if he was in a hurry for something. He hoped it wasn't to get Elsie into trouble again. Alex looked towards Elsie and nearly said something. However, she looked like she was having a good time laughing with Josh. Alex considered what Elsie had said to him about Josh being distant lately. Alex thought that it was a better idea to tell Elsie later.

They finally arrived at a beautiful two storey home with a large front yard that had trees in all shapes and sizes of unicorns, trolls, dogs, cats and rabbits. Small floating lights were flying and circling around the large flowers that bloomed in the gardens.

"Come on," said Juliana, as she walked up to the large rose wooden door and placed her hand on a circular indent in the door, which then glowed a dull forest green. The door opened up revealing a long dark green corridor.

Alex looked at Elsie. She was no longer happy and seemed to be troubled, trying her hardest not to show it. However, Alex could see straight through the delicate front, which she was working so hard to acquire. He could see it so palpable in her eyes.

Alex followed everyone through the narrow corridor with large family portraits hanging on the walls, through an archway and into a large lounge room in which he sat upon one of the soft white couches. Juliana walked around the room pulling curtains closed then sat down.

"Ok now that no one can hear or see us. Josh, how are we going to do this?"

"I'm not quite sure, I never really thought that part through."

"You're lucky I have an idea," replied Juliana.

"How?" asked Elsie, still looking worried.

"I was sort of expecting this to happen. I have been dreading it. My mother told me once of this secret pathway" Juliana took in a big breath, let it out slowly then continued "Mother use to tell me stories about it when I was a little girl, but as I got older, I forgot all about it... Until... one day when I was out in the back yard, I was bored. So bored that I began thinking strange and unusual thoughts and one of them was, why is it that everyone has hedges in their backyards?"

Everyone looked at Juliana in puzzlement.

"What's that got to do with...," began Josh.

"Well, has anyone ever went past them?"

"Past them? I've walked past them all the time. What's that got to do with anything?"

"No... not past them, as such..., I mean..., Through them, yes Through Them! Has anyone ever walked through a hedge?"

Josh laughed. "The only reason we would want to do that is if we had a death wish. The only thing on the other side of those hedges is the mist!"

"Shh. Josh... let her finish, what about them? What happened?" Elsie asked, intrigued.

"Well, I was out there thinking about the hedges and looking at them when all of a sudden I heard this small voice and I felt something sharp prick my leg. I jumped back and I saw this thing stuck to my leg, so I pulled it out and threw it away. The next second, I heard more voices yelling and screaming. I fell into the bush and this little person stood on the middle of my forehead holding a long spear. He said to me, 'You, human, leave us be. We knew you would someday come and start a war on our gnome civilisation. What have you done with my daughter?' And this other woman, well gnome as they call themselves, came out and said, 'And my son? What have you done with my son?' So, I struggled to stand up straight and… well…"

"What? What happened?" asked Elsie, in excitement.

"Well… I fell through the hedge!!!!"

Everyone looked at Juliana in shock.

"Why didn't you tell me? Why haven't you said anything?" asked Elsie,

"I haven't finished yet."

"Ok."

"So, I ended up on some pathway. The gnomes were throwing spears at me, I was in shock and scared, so I ran for it!"

"Where did you go?" asked Alex.

"I didn't know where I was going. I was just thinking about getting away and I was thinking about how I really wished that Elsie was there to help me. Then all of a sudden, I heard your voice, Elsie."

"My voice?"

"Yeah, I heard your voice and I looked over the hedge and I was outside your backyard. You must have been yelling out at Brandon or something, so I quickly jumped over the hedge and ran home. I didn't say anything because I thought you would think I was making it up and honestly, I didn't know what to think of it myself and that's not all of it! When

I arrived home, it was hours later, and I only felt like I was gone for about 15 minutes. My mother was furious.”

“Wow that's cool and just think we will be able to go on that path any time we want to,” Josh said, in amazement.

Elsie looked worried. “How do you know it is safe? I mean they must have put the hedges there for a reason, right?”

“Don't worry, I'll protect you. Nothing will go wrong,” said Josh, as he put his arm around Elsie's shoulders.

Juliana's backyard looked almost like the front yard. “So how do we get to the pathway?”

“It's over here,” said Juliana, walking across the yard and past the clothesline which was shaking birds off its lines. Garden tools were huddled into a corner making clunking sounds to each other. Then past a large shrub that had been shaped into a lifelike woman with long hair, wearing a knee height, windswept dress, in the centre of the backyard.

“Who is that?” asked Alex.

“It's Juliana's Mother” whispered Elsie looking sad. Making sure Juliana was nowhere near, she took a deep breath and continued. “She died, about five years ago. Mrs Winter was an amazing woman. Extremely kind and had a great imagination. She used to sit down with us when we were little and tell us all wonderful stories. She was a very thin, fragile lady.”

"So where is this pathway?" They could hear Josh asking as they approached the back of the yard.

Chapter 11. Hedges

Alex could see a long, tall, red and green-leafed shrub stretched across from one side of the yard to the other and above was a transparent grey, white and dark grey mist swirling around.

A small voice yelled out as they approached. "I have been waiting for you Juliana. You have not come anywhere near us for the last four years. What do you think you are doing here this time? Have you come to wreck another family, destroy our homes or start a war?" The gnome looked angry and upset.

"I didn't. I really didn't do that. I felt something hurt my leg and I fell in and couldn't get back out. When I tried, I fell straight through the other side. I am terribly sorry for your home, but I really didn't mean it".

A gnome woman came running out with her hands waving in the air yelling at the top of her little voice. "Do you know what you've done! Do you know what you have done to our family? To our home and most importantly, to our SON AND DAUGHTER!! Where are they? You…. you Giant! You… You HUMAN!"

"I don't. I don't know what you're talking about." frowned Juliana with tears starting to form in her eyes.

"You know what happened to them you must! They have disappeared ever since you came along and destroyed our home. Do you know what it feels like? What it feels like to wake up every morning and see my own daughter's empty bed," said the lady, as tears ran down her little face.

Juliana was crying as well, "Yes," she sniffled. "I do know. My mum died 5 years ago. I know how you feel. I dont know what I did. I am so sorry."

"Truly, she didn't do it on purpose Sir and Mam," said Alex.

"Really she didn't," said Elsie.

"Is this right, Juliana? Would you stake your life on it?" asked the man gnome, as he wiped away a tear from his cheek.

"Yes, yes, I would. I have no reason to wreck your home, Sir," replied Juliana, knowing that a gnome does not give up on revenge that easily.

"Well... Alright then... So, what are you here for this time?" Juliana looked at him in shock.

"We are heading to The Rottingwood tonight for Halloween, sir and we would like to ask if we can pass through to the path please?" asked Alex.

"On one condition."

Juliana looked at the gnome concerned. She knew gnomes didn't give up so easily.

"What is it?" asked Alex.

"You must take me with you to Rottingwood. I want to find my daughter and Mrs Johnson's son, but you cannot say anything to anyone about me going with you. Is it a deal?"

Alex looked back at Josh, Elsie and Juliana. Josh shrugged. Elsie made a I don't know look on her face and Juliana said, "Ok. It's a deal. It was my fault it happened so I should be the one to help."

"Ok then, it's a deal, Juliana," said the little man. Then he held out his hand with what looked to be a large blackberry,

"Uh."

"You take it and eat it."

"Why?"

"Because it seals our deal. It's a gnome's honour berry. If you eat this, it means no matter what, you have to keep your word. If you don't... Well...,"

"What?"

"The berry will become poisonous and kill you." Juliana stared at the gnome. "It will kill me?"

"Oh, is that all??" said Josh, rolling his eyes being sarcastic

"Well... yes".

"No, you can't do it!" said Elsie. "We will find another way in!"

"No…, no, it's… it's ok. I will do it. I have no intention of breaking my word. My word is my honour."

She took the berry in her hand and swallowed it.

"Julie! No!" yelled Elsie. Everyone stared at her like she was going to drop dead that very second.

A few minutes past.

"I'm not dead, so, come on, let's go. Where do you want to sit for the ride, Mr Johnson?"

The gnome laughed. "No, no, no, me and Mrs Johnson are just friends, nothing else."

"Oh, right."

"You can call me Sim."

"Ok Sim. Where would you like to sit?"

"That backpack you are wearing looks like it could be comfy." Juliana took off her backpack and opened the front pocket. "How about here?"

"Looks fine to me, just a second," replied Sim and walked off into the shrub. About five minutes later he came back with a blanket, a stick with a sack tied to the end of it and what looked to be a small jar with water in it.

"Ok I'm all ready," he said, looking up at Julie. She opened her bag again. Sim jumped into the small front pocket of her backpack and she put it on her back.

"Hang on a minute. He didn't tell us how to get through," stated Josh.

A murmur came from inside the backpack, then they heard a zzzzzziiiiiipppp. "Oh, sorry about that." Julie turned around and they could all see Sim poking his head out of the pocket.

"How do we do this?" asked Josh.

"If you want to get through the hedge, you must think of where you want to be when you get to the other side. Then the hedge will open for you to go through. Be very careful when you get to the other side as we have no way of knowing what or who will be over there when you get to the other side. It can be very.. dangerous."

"Oh great. Just the thing we need, more danger. So... who is going to go first?" asked Josh.

They all looked at each other. Then Elsie said "How about you Josh, since this was all your idea."

"I suppose. I am the bravest amongst us." Josh looks over at Alex with a glint in his eye.

"Alright. Think of a path on the other side, nothing else, just a path," said Sim. Josh closed his eyes, visioning walking through the hedge to a pathway. "I see it in my mind."

"Now vision the hedge opening up and letting you walk through," replied Sim. All of a sudden, the hedge began to untangle itself to make a path through to the other side.

"Open your eyes and walk through."

Josh opened his eyes and took a step towards the hedge, then another step and another. The hedge started to grow back together as he got closer. "Keep the thought firmly in your mind! Or it will encase you or even strangle you to death!"

"NOW YOU TELL ME!" yelled Josh as he tried to concentrate harder.

He walked through quickly onto a pathway on the other side. The hedge began winding back together again. "Oh wow!" They could hear Josh on the other side.

"Are you ok over there?" asked Elsie.

"Yeah, this is cool. All I see is a long pathway, a VERY long pathway."

"Ok, I'll go next," said Juliana. She closed her eyes, and the hedge began to untangle itself. Juliana walked through and the hedge closed. Elsie could hear her speaking from the other side. "Well, that was easier than I thought it would be, your turn Elsie."

Elsie closed her eyes and waited... Opened her eyes, the hedge was still there. She closed them again and tried hard to concentrate. "I can't seem to vision it," she opened her eyes and looked at Alex.

"Maybe try thinking about what the other side would look like? Or what it looked like when the hedge was opening up for them. Would you prefer if I went first?"

Elsie took a deep breath. "No, it's ok, I'll be fine."

"Alright, I will be right behind you if you need me, ok?"

Elsie looked into Alex's eyes, nodded, closed her eyes and took in deep breaths thinking to herself, 'it's ok Elsie you can do it. Just vision the hedge opening, the leaves parting the pathway leading through it'. She took more deep breaths.

"Elsie! Are you Alright?" yelled Juliana.

"Yeah, just focusing."

"It's working!" said Alex, as he watched the leaves tremble, move, then the hedge began to part.

"I did it!" said Elsie, opening her eyes. "I'm scared! I don't want to walk through it."

"I'll come with you!" Alex walked up beside Elsie and held onto her hand. They slowly walked through the hedge together.

"Ok let's go," said Josh, glaring at Alex.

"I... I feel strange and tingly all over," said Juliana.

"You can lean on my shoulder," said Alex, as he moved towards her.

"My feet, they feel, heavy." she tried lifting her foot, but it just wouldn't move. It wouldn't budge. All of a sudden, the ground under her started to shake and went a crimson red. "What's happening," she trembled almost falling over.

"I don't know," replied Alex, grabbing her arm to hold her up. "My... My feet are sinking!" yelled Juliana. "Help me!"

Alex held her tight as she started to sink quickly. The ground began to glow bright. "It's pulling me down! Help!" The land was cracking.

Elsie gasped loudly as she saw long thin scaled green arms with hands reaching up out of the cracks grasping at Julie's legs. Alex had to move, or it would pull him in as well. He held onto Juliana's hand, tightly refusing to let go. "I'm Falling! I'm Falling! Help Me!"

Juliana's hand was getting sweaty and starting to slip "No! No! Don't let go!" All they could see now was the top half of her body. Her hand slipped.

Alex quickly looked around trying to find something for her to hold onto. "Alex! she is sinking really fast!" yelled Elsie. Alex closed his eyes. "This is no time for sleep, Alex!" yelled Elsie.

"If only I had a rope! If only I had a rope! IF I HAD A ROPE!" he started shouting loudly. "IF I HAD A ROPE! IF I HAD A ROPE" He started rocking back and forth with his eyes closed "A ROPE! A ROPE! A ROPE!"

Then Alex opened his eyes and there in front of him laid a rope. He grabbed the end of the rope and through the other end to Juliana.

"I... I can't reach it!" she cried, tears running down her face. The green hands were all over her.

She was just about suffocating. "Come on! Come on!!" yelled Alex.

The rope started to get longer as he concentrated. It began to weave itself longer and longer.

Juliana grabbed the rope now gasping for air. Alex quickly pulled on the rope. Josh and Elsie grabbed the rope as well, pulling her up and out of the hole. Juliana collapsed into Alex's arms crying. Elsie watched the hole as it began to close.

"What the hell just happened!" said Josh.

"I don't know, but I'm starting to regret coming here," replied Elsie, wiping tears from her eyes, looking at Juliana. Juliana let go of Alex and flopped onto the ground next to Elsie's feet with tears still running down her cheeks. She looked up at Alex. "I don't know what I would have done without you. You saved my life" Alex sat down next to her and wiped away the tears not knowing what to say. He was shocked at what had just happened.

"Are you ok?" asked Elsie, kneeling down beside her. "I... I think so. Just... Just a little scared."

"That is to be expected," said Josh, sitting down with them.

"Are you sure you still want to do this" asked Elsie, feeling more scared about going now then she had been before.

"I don't know, I, I don't want anything else to happen to us," Juliana said, wiping away the rest of her tears.

"Where is your backyard? I can't see it. How would we know where it is?" asked Elsie.

"Uhm...,"

All they could see was a long, tall line of hedges and on the other side of the pathway was the wall of mist.

"SIM!" startled Alex as he looked at Juliana's back, realising that her backpack wasn't there.

"Oh NO! He's gone!" She looked up at them scared. "You'll be ok Julie," replied Elsie, looking worried.

"There's no way of getting back. I guess we have no choice, we have to continue," said Josh.

Everyone nodded in agreement.

"Let's stick together and make our way there," said Alex, putting his arm around Juliana for support as she stood up. They all started walking slowly together down the pathway. They passed a group of large trees, a few shrubs with flowers, some more trees and a tree that looked very old with its large roots sticking out of the ground. There wasn't much to look at. They walked a bit faster.

"I think it's around this corner," said Juliana, as they passed another big tree. They walked around the corner passed a shrub. "Maybe it's this corner coming up," replied Josh.

They walked a bit faster, past more trees, shrubs, then around the corner and there was another big tree.

"Does that look like the same tree to you Elsie?" asked Alex.

"No.., I don't think it is. It looks a bit like it, but I don't think it is."

"Ok," They walked further up the pathway and there was another corner.

Chapter 12. Simulcast

They walked further up the pathway along the tall hedges and there was another small shrub, then a group of trees, then a shrub around another corner.

"Am I the only person who thinks we are walking in circles?" asked Alex.

"I think we are," replied Juliana, who went and sat next to the hedges.

"I'm stuffed," said Josh.

"Me to," replied Elsie, sitting next to the hedge,

Alex went and sat next to Julie. "I think this was a bad idea to come here."

"So do I," said Juliana.

"I don't," said Josh.

"You never think any of your ideas are bad, Josh," replied Elsie, looking angry.

"Well, I don't see you coming up with anything," replied Josh, now getting upset.

"Stop it the both of you," Juliana said, hugging her knees.

"No Julie, you're the one who came up with this stupid idea of going through these damn hedges," replied Josh, pacing back and forth. Juliana started to cry.

"Now look what you've done," said Alex, putting his arm around her. Elsie went red in the face looking at Alex hugging Juliana. "So... You two have a thing going on now, do you?" she said in spite.

"Why? Why do you think that?" asked Alex, upset.

"Well, you're getting that close to her you might as well kiss her!" said Elsie, going bright red.

"So what, so what if I did? Is there something wrong with that? Does that change anything? We are still stuck out here in the middle of nowhere!"

"Then go on, get it over and done with so we can move on and you don't have to hide it anymore. Kiss her then and get it over and done with!" yelled Elsie, standing up and storming off along the pathway.

"I don't want him to kiss me!" yelled Juliana back at Elsie Alex pulled his arm back from around her and moved over away from Juliana.

"You don't want to kiss me, do you?" asked Juliana, looking at Alex.

"Uh... I... no... No, I don't."

"So... so I'm not good enough for you? Is it because you're completely in love with Elsie?"

"I never said that!" said Alex, standing up.

"That's ok I didn't want to kiss you in the first place," said Juliana, hiding her head with her arms over her knees.

"You guys! Guys! Stop fighting," yelled Josh running up in front of Elsie.

"It's magic. I know it is, I… I can see it… Can't you? Look!" He pointed into the air.

They all walked up to Josh trying to see what he was talking about.

"I… I can see it too," said Alex, as a soft bluish mist started to appear in front of him and he then noticed that they were all breathing it in.

"Cover your nose and mouth!" yelled Alex.

They quickly covered their nose and mouths, except for Juliana who stormed up to Josh and said, "Stupid excuse."

"It's true, just listen to me!"

Juliana slapped him in the face.

"You listen to this! You think you're too good for anyone nowadays. I wish I had never met you."

Josh being so angry with fury stormed up the pathway. 'CRASH,' suddenly someone ran straight into him sending Josh backwards onto his backside. "Ahh! What the hell!" he said, still full of anger.

Elsie, Alex and Juliana hid behind the shrub as much as they could.

"What on earth are you doing? Don't you know who I am?" the person said, as Josh stood up straight and brushed himself off. "I am Brandon. You don't want any trouble, do you? You really should have a bit more respect for people better than yourself!"

"Huh? oh... Brandon, it's you, sorry. What are you doing out here?" Josh asked, feeling his anger turn into nervous tension.

"I'm going for a run. I need to tone up my muscles. Where is Elsie?"

Josh was trying to think of what to say. He could either tell Brandon that Elsie was right here with him or he can make up an excuse.

Elsie froze behind the shrub staring at Josh, hoping he wouldn't say anything. She was regretting what she had mentioned to Josh earlier.

"She is at Juliana's house watching Halloween movies. I will be going back there soon, just getting a few drinks. Do you want me to give her a message?".

Elsie sighed quietly in relief and was very grateful.

"Just tell Elsie that I am going with my friends to the new space dome that she always wanted to see. She will want to kill me when she finds out." Brandon laughed, snorted, then ran off with his bulges wobbling. Josh waited until he could no longer see Brandon.

"What muscles? He doesn't even have a brain, how could he have muscles?" Elsie walked out from behind the shrub. "Thank you so much, Josh. You didn't have to lie to him, but I am really, really glad you did. Thank you, I am so sorry for what I said before."

"It's alright," replied Josh, blushing. "I understand. Everything is a bit muddled up around here."

Juliana and Alex walked out from behind the shrub as well. Juliana hung her head low and said, "I didn't really mean It... I really didn't." She put her head up and looked at Josh continuing to say, "It must have been the hedges making us fight. That's why the gnomes are so nasty. I'm so sorry for what I did. Could you ever forgive me? If you don't... I understand...," She hung her head low again.

"It's alright Julie, I forgive you. We just need to stay away from those nasty hedges, and I do realise I have changed a lot in the past few weeks and I'm sorry. I just have had a lot going on at the moment, but I will it make it up to you all, even you Alex."

"And I'm sorry too. I shouldn't have said the things I said," Alex gave Elsie and Juliana a hug.

Elsie looked at them all and said, "And I am sorry. You are all my best friends. I wouldn't trade you guys for anything" They all smiled.

"Ok, ok, that's enough mushy stuff" laughed Josh. "Let's get a move on." They started walking again but this time seemed different. There were flowers on the sides of the path that they did not notice last time and it felt like they were actually getting somewhere.

"I can't believe it! I think we are nearly there!" said Josh, eagerly.

"Yay, we finely made it woohoo!" Juliana yelled out loud, pointing to a large yard with dead trees and big ugly birds flying around.

"Yep, I knew we could do it," said Alex.

"It's bizarre. I am looking forward to seeing The Rottingwood," said Elsie.

"Me to," replied Juliana.

Alex looked around. "Oh look! I can see it now!"

"Yep... this must be it," said Elsie.

"So, is everyone ready? Are you ready Elsie?" asked Josh, looking over at Elsie.

"Yes! I am totally ready now. I can't believe I am finally ready, but I am. I am finely ready to face The Rottingwood. I mean..., I don't think it will be as bad as they say. I think it's all just a myth."

"I'm ready. I really want to know what all the fuss is," said Alex.

"Ok, here goes nothing. I wonder if these gnomes are as nasty as the others," said Josh, looking at the long hedge in front of them, then taking a few steps forward clearing his throat."A' hum, a, A' hum" nothing happens. Josh coughs louder "A' hum, A' hum!" nothing happens.

Alex looks around the shrubs, looking for some sign of gnomes when noticing the shrub didn't quite look right, Alex bent forward to take a closer look at the branches "Broken."

"What was that?" asked Josh.

"Broken," stated Alex as he stood up straight.

"What are you talking about?"

"These branches, if you take a closer look at the shrub, a lot of the branches and twigs are all snapped and broken and look at the leaves, it's like as if someone has been crunching them up in their hands. They are all wrinkled. There is green runny stuff coming out of some and there is sap seeping out of the bark."

Elsie reached out and held onto one of the leaves. She touched the green liquid that was leaking from a cut "Blood."

"Blood?" questioned Alex.

"Yes blood, this poor shrub has been attacked. It has blood leaking from its cuts. I can see some of its veins have been cut."

"Listen…., Shh… Listen," said Alex, putting his hand to his ear. All went quiet for a few minutes as Alex softly moved some of the leaves here and there.

"Alex, I don't hear anything," said Juliana.

"It's coming from……" He moved the leaves until he found a small brown, what looked to be a bird's nest "From here." He picked up the tiny nest and looked inside. "I can hear it more now."

"Me too," said Juliana and Josh.

"It, it sounds like breathing," said Elsie.

Alex slowly slid his hand into the nest and pulled it back out. In the palm of his hand, curled up in a tiny ball, was what appeared to be a little childlike gnome. It was wearing a pink dress with a large pink bow at the back.

"She, she's crying," said Elsie.

Alex slowly ran his little finger over the soft brown fluffy hair on the gnomes' head.

The little girl flinched and curled up even tighter. "It's ok little one, we won't hurt you."

The little girl looked up at Alex and he noticed she had a tiny pacifier in her mouth.

"Where are your mummy and daddy little one?"

All of a sudden "OUCH! MY LEG" Alex quickly put the little girl into the nest and put her back. Then reached down to his leg. There was a tiny bit of stick about the size of a toothpick sticking out of his calf. He bent down and yanked it out.

"LEAVE MY LITTLE SISTER ALONE!"

"Who said that?" Alex looked around to see where the small male voice was coming from.

"Over here," said Julie, pointing to a little boy standing in the bottom of the shrub.

"You leave my sister alone!" yelled the gnome boy.

"What happened here," asked Julie.

"What's it to you? For all I know, you're in league with him!"

"With whom"

"The Simulcast."

"Oh no..." said Elsie, in dismay

"What? What is it?" asked Alex.

"The Simulcast, bad news," replied Elsie.

"But what is it?"

"It's not what is it, it's who is it," said Josh and continued, "And I bet I know exactly who it is."

"Sim," said Elsie and Juliana.

"Sim? What? What is he?" asked Alex.

The small boy looked up at Alex with sadness, devastation and anger in his eyes and said, "The Simulcast casts itself off to be a gnome when really it's something else entirely. The Simulcast only ever has one thing on its mind, that is destruction and immense knowledge of destruction. It only comes out once every five hundred years and when it does, you can only guess at what happens."

"Is there anything we can do?" asked Alex.

"Nothing, absolutely nothing, once it has started there is no way to stop it. You must let it run its course."

"Is there anything we can do to help you?"

"No, we will be fine. Everyone is in with the healers. We just have to wait."

"Can, can we get through the hedge?" asked Josh.

"Yes, just be careful that you don't get hurt from the injured limbs."

"Thank you, I hope you all return to full health," said Juliana.

"I hope so too. Take care on your journey," said the boy, as he walked into the hedge and disappeared.

One by one, they each walked carefully through the opening in the hedge, making sure not to get scratched by the protruding branches. Once on the other side, all they could see were lots of dead trees. They heard a loud 'screech.'

"We better get going before it gets too late," said Josh, as he leads them into the trees.

It was dark and gloomy, dead trees surrounded them and all they could hear were loud squawks coming from above.

"This is spooky," said Juliana.

"I know what you mean," replied Elsie.

"Where should we go now?" asked Alex.

"I'm going to look over there, just wait here." Josh pointed east towards a large clump of trees.

"Don't be a long time..., please," said Juliana, worried.

"I won't," he replied, as he strolled off into the large clump of trees.

Alex sat on a large stump. "This all feels like I am dreaming."

"I wish we never came here," said Juliana, as she sat on the ground and put her arms around herself.

"Maybe we should just go home if we can," said Elsie, looking around at all the trees as she knelt down and placed her arm around Juliana's shoulders.

"We should," replied Juliana.

'SQUAWK!'

They all looked upwards Elsie and Juliana screamed. A huge black crow was swooping down on them. "Quick run!" yelled Alex.

The bird swooped down at them reaching out its clawed feet at Juliana's head. She screamed.

"This way!" Yelled Alex pointing towards a clearing in the trees.

They ran as fast as they could. Alex looked back as he was running. The bird was swooping down on them again. "FASTER! IT'S CATCHING UP!"

Juliana screamed a high pitch scream as the bird held some of her hair in its clenched sharp claw and pulled as threads of her long blond hair came out. The bird swooped upwards then back down at her again. Elsie grabbed Juliana's hand and ran faster. Juliana let go and ran in a different direction.

"NOOOOO!" yelled Elsie as she watched Juliana run off with the bird following her.

"We have to find them. We can't just leave them here Alex," said Elsie, breathless and looking worried.

"Julie! Julie! Josh! Josh!" they called out with no response, walking around the trees looking for Josh and Juliana. Alex looked up trees and under shrubs but there was no sign of either one. There was a scream. "Who was that? Elsie?"

Alex looked around and couldn't see anyone "Hello??? Elsie! Where did you go?" There was no answer from anyone, "What could I do? Try and find them? Go back to the hedge? I don't think I could find the hedge now even if I wanted to" Alex said to himself. There was a flapping noise like wings. He looked up into the sky and could see the bird.

"Coming back for more, are you?!" Alex yelled up at the bird. "Well, you're not going to get me!" He started running, then looked back, the bird swooped down. It seemed almost half his size. Its beak sharp. Alex ran as fast as he could. The bird started squawking loudly. There was a house ahead. He ran faster. Something hit him. He fell backwards, hit his head on a rock, and then everything went dark.

Chapter 13. Rottingwood

"Alex, Alex," said a small voice. Alex slowly opened his eyes. He was laying on his back on the ground.

"Alex! Alex!" His vision was blurry. There were lots of bright colours coming from his chest, but it was all so blurry. He felt a weight on his chest. Things started to become more apparent. He could see something small and colourful on his chest.

"Kitten," he said softly.

"What?" the voice said.

"Kitten?" then the image became more transparent. The colours were disappearing. "Don't go."

"I'm not going anywhere," the voice said, now a bit deeper than before.

"Who? Who are you kitten?"

"I don't know who kitten is, Alex. But it's me EELLLS SIIIIIEEE…"

All of a sudden, Elsie's voice came out loud and clear "Ok, ok, I can hear you, Ouch!"

Alex grabbed the top of his head in pain. Elsie had her hand on his chest, while leaning over him trying to wake him up.

"Alex, are you ok? I was worried about you."

" What happened?" Asked Alex

"I was calling out for Juliana and I heard someone yelling. I thought it might have been Josh. That's when I bumped into you. Well you bumped into me. Ran straight into me and then we fell backwards and we hit our heads on this concrete step." She pointed to a step that lay beneath his head. "Alex, did you see Juliana or Josh?"

"No, I was hoping you did."

"I haven't seen them, but I think we should find out if anyone is home. They might be able to help us."

Alex stood up and knocked on the door, looking ragged and tired from the run. They could hear footsteps heading towards them. The door started to open, and a head poked around the corner with long wavy grey hair.

"Miss Borrow!" said Elsie, surprised.

Miss Borrow opened the door the rest of the way. "I have been waiting for you, come in, you look exhausted."

"Juliana and Josh...," Elsie began to say but was cut off by Miss Borrow. "It's ok, they will be fine. All will be explained soon enough."

Miss Borrow led them into the lounge room. "Have a seat. I will get you both a drink," she said, pointing to three soft emerald couches positioned around a glass coffee table, with emerald coasters and a golden candelabra. Large portrait paintings were placed around the walls. On the floor lay a dark emerald carpet with light emerald designs. A stone fireplace was located opposite them. The high wooden roof had feathers and chimes hanging down. Alex and Elsie were both feeling very much in a daze after what had happened. Elsie remembered what her mum had said about the house.

"I hope mum doesn't find out," she said, looking over at Alex sitting on the couch next to her. "Don't worry, she won't," he replied, looking around thinking how enormous the room looked compared to the outside of the house.

Miss Borrow walked in with three glasses filled with a rainbow liquid. The liquid looked as if it was swirling around the glass. "What is that?" questioned Alex. "This drink is called Energy Swirl. It gives you energy and makes you feel better," she said, putting the glasses on the table in front of them then sat down.

Alex picked up his glass looked at Elsie, shrugged his shoulders then took a big gulp.

"Mmm, tastes like strawberry." He took another sip, "And now it tastes like pineapple." Elsie thought to herself 'Well, Alex looks ok, I might as well try some'.

She took a sip. It tasted like blueberry. "Wow it works straight away. I'm starting to feel better already. What's it made of?" asked Elsie, taking another sip. Miss Borrow looked at them and said, "Well as I said before, I've been waiting for you. I have a secret I want to share. I know you are both trustworthy and can keep this to yourselves." She stood up and led them to a long painted picture on the wall of bright green vines. Miss Borrow touched the centre of the picture with the tip of her pointer finger. The vines began to move.

"Wow," said Alex. They were like slithering snakes glowing and forming a door. Some of them gathered together, raised out of the wall and created a handle. Miss Borrow turned the handle. The door opened. The sound and smell of a waterfall breezed into the room. There was a wall of flowing water. Alex could see their reflection.

"Follow me," said Miss Borrow, stepping through the water. Elsie looked at Alex. The water had him spellbound. Alex stretched out his arm and touched the water with his finger.

"Uh!" He jumped back and looked at his finger. Elsie went over to him and quickly looked at his finger.

"Oh Alex. There's nothing wrong with it, you scaredy-cat," she laughed. Alex laughed at himself. "Well, it was tingly."

"If you don't go, I will."

"Ok, ok I'll go." He stretched out his arm slowly and put his hand through.

"What are you doing!?" Miss Borrows head popped out of the water and nearly head-butted Alex. He jumped backwards and fell over. Elsie and Miss Borrow laughed "Well. What are you waiting for, come in," said Miss Borrow.

"Ok, ok, I was just about to," said Alex.

Miss Borrow's head went back in. Alex looked at Elsie and said, "Ok I'm going, I'm going." He walked through the water quickly. Elsie went through slowly. The water was beautiful. It was tingly, refreshing and she wasn't getting wet.

"Oh my…., I have been dreaming of this place!" said Alex, in amazement while looking around at all the unusual creatures, flowers, trees and shrubs talking, walking and flying around with people in all different sizes. They spoke a language that Alex had never heard before. It was like a world inside a world. There was no roof or ceiling, only bright blue sky and green grass. Alex turned around and saw the door floating in mid-air. "Miss… uh….," said Alex, as he looked around and noticed Miss Borrow standing in front of a Bookstand that held a thick Book. Her dress was now long blue and made out of silk. Her hair was long blonde, with ringlets. She was young and there was no bird pinned on her shoulder, instead there was a real baby phoenix pruning itself.

Miss Borrow looked up at them. "So what do you think?"

"I, I can't believe my own eyes. It's beautiful! Where are we?" asked Elsie.

"Fabilchi."

Alex tried to pronounce the name, "Fabi... Fabial... Fabialchie."

"Fabilchi, this place preserves youth and beauty. No one would ever believe that I am 250 years old, would they?" asked Miss Borrow.

"250!?, that's..., uh...," said Alex, trying not to be rude. Alex was looking at something in a box.

"Old," said Miss Borrow and laughed.

"Yeah but you still look really young for your age."

"In here I do," replied Miss Borrow, continuing to read her Book. Elsie walked over to see what Alex was looking at. She looked in the box and saw two rainbow kittens, one with blue eyes, one with dark green eyes and eight tiny kittens about the same size of a small child's thumb. "Hello Alex and Elsie," said the blue-eyed kitten.

"You can talk?" said Elsie.

"Yes, my name is Chary, and this is my husband Benevolent. These little ones are my babies."

"So, you must be an adult? cat?" asked Alex.

"My husband and I are both cats. However, in your world, we would be known as kittens."

"So, you don't grow any bigger?"

"We won't grow any bigger, though we do come in many different sizes" Benevolent and Chary let out a short laugh.

"What's funny?"

"Oh, just a little joke between my husband and me."

"Have you two finished exploring?" asked Miss Borrow, waving at them to come over to her, then continued to say, "This is where I live and everything here has a magical energy field even more potent than the mist, but you will learn about that later. You both have been chosen by the Spirit Gia Of Nature to come here for some reason. I'm not quite sure what that reason is but whatever reason, it must be necessary. We haven't had anyone here for over thirty years. Gia's message to me was for you to come in and experience the elements, plant life, creatures of legend, magic and wisdom. There are a lot of different beings here that you have never seen or heard of before. I don't know why the Spirit Of Nature has chosen you two, but whatever she says is the law. Gia is the essence of wisdom and all life as we know it. Without Gia, none of us would be alive today. Here are two portals." Miss Borrow handed Alex and Elsie a clear crystal each and said, "You are to keep these crystals with you at all times. Put them in your pockets for now.

If you lose them, don't worry you will find them, when you want to come back to Fabilchi just say the words' saga, chi, clandestine'. Make sure the crystals are in front of you when you say it."

"I can't remember that," said Alex.

"Don't worry about remembering it. Don't worry about anything, you are welcome here any time you like," said Miss Borrow. Alex started to feel very light-headed, the sun was getting brighter like someone was shining a bright light into his eyes. It was getting brighter and brighter.

"Miss.., Mis...," Alex was trying to get her attention.

He could hear Miss Borrow still talking softly, "Anytime, anytime you like, Alex...,"

"Miss, I can't see you."

"Alex... Alex!" He could hear her calling him. "I can't, Miss.... I can't see you."

"Alex... Alex...,"

"I'm... Here..., I just can't."

"Get UP! ALEX!" replied Hazel.

"Oh..., Sorry Mrs McKormick," he said, squinting his eyes up at her.

"Why didn't I see you and Elsie come in last night? I was worried about you, I looked at the door stepometer this morning and it says you got home at twenty minutes past nine?"

"I'm, I'm not sure, Sorry."

"Well, get ready for school, or you will be late. Elsie should know better than to keep you out all night."

"Yes Mam," he replied, as Mrs McKormick walked out of the room closing the door.

Alex sat on the side of the bed and looked at himself in a mirror that was half-covered up underneath everything. He looked horrid. His hair was all messy and frizzy, eyes puffy from being tired and his clothing wrinkled from sleeping in them.

"The crystal," he said to himself, as he slipped his hand into his pocket and pulled out a small pebble that looked like something you would find in a garden, black and brown with white writing on it saying, saga, chi, clandestine.

"It really happened…, except it's a pebble, not a crystal." He got dressed for school, placed the pebble in his bag and went out into the dining room for breakfast.

In the dining room, only Elsie and her mother were sitting at the table. There was a plate with two pieces of toast placed in front of Alex's chair.

"Quickly Alex! I've set your breakfast, come sit and eat, no time to waste!" said Hazel.

Alex sat at the table and ate quickly.

"Elsie, you still didn't tell me what happened last night. Your father and I were so worried. You shouldn't have kept Alex out all night like that. You never know what might have happened. You could have been eaten by some sort of creature or attacked by a thief. Anything could have happened."

"I... We...,"

"Finished!" said Alex, quickly shoving the last of his toast into his mouth to break up the awkward moment. "May we go mum?" asked Elsie.

"Ok but you will have to tell me sooner or later. Don't dawdle. Get to school as soon as you can. You hear me?"

"Yes mum." Elsie and Alex said goodbye and went outside where Juliana was waiting for them. Juliana looked so excited. "That was a great night! We were given lots of candy. I can't believe we went to every house! Well, except for The Rottingwood. It was so fun! Especially when we went to the milkshake and Josh spilt that drink all over himself!" she laughed.

"Uh... yeah... it was...," said Elsie, trying to make herself laugh. "Uh... we did?" asked Alex, quietly looking over at Elsie. Elsie shrugged her shoulders.

When they got to school Josh and Lilly were waiting under the lucky tree. Lilly looked like she usually did, flirting with Josh. Josh looking uncomfortable as usual.

"Can I talk to you?" asked Josh, looking at Elsie.

"Uh…, Sure," she replied, looking confused.

Josh stood up and walked over to where Elsie was standing alone. "Is this about last night?" asked Elsie.

"Yeah…, Something really strange is going on."

"You remember?"

"Of course, I remember. How couldn't I remember last night…?"

"Well I thought, Julie, well she said…,"

Josh cut in on her talking and said, "Shh. I have to tell you this quickly…,"

"What?"

"Lilly tried to kiss me last night and I shoved a pie in my mouth so she couldn't."

Elsie burst out laughing. "Hahaha really?"

Josh laughed as well. "Ha-ha yeah, Shh… I was kind of hoping you would be there to save me as usual, but you were not." Elsie stopped laughing. "I wasn't?"

"No…, I hoped you would have come to my rescue like you always do, but you were not there."

"Oh…, uh…, sorry…, well… where was I?" asked Elsie, feeling awkward. "You should know ha-ha! You went home with Alex because you felt sick, remember? I'm guessing you were very sick since you can't remember very well. Actually, you still don't look too well. I really missed you when you left last night. I hope you are feeling a bit better today."

"Oh, right yeah..., I am still feeling a bit sick, but I'm sure I will feel better soon."

"Yeah," replied Josh, scratching his head now feeling awkward. "So what's the big secret?" asked Lilly, coming up behind Josh and grabbing hold of his arm with both of her hands like she didn't want him to run away.

"Oh nothing, I just thought I'd ask Elsie if she could help me with my homework."

"I could help you," said Lilly, looking jealous.

"Oh..., uh..., it's ok now. I didn't realise. I didn't need to do it after all."

Lilly gave Elsie a suspicious look, turned away grabbed her bag and walked off.

"I don't know why she gets so jealous of me. it's not like she's my girlfriend or anything," said Josh, confused.

"Don't worry about Lilly. She goes through these fazes, you know that."

"I suppose so," replied Josh, now going a shade of red.

"Hey Elsie!" yelled Alex sitting under the tree by himself.

"I'll see you in class Elsie," said Josh, turning to head off to class.

Elsie went and sat next to him. "What happened last night?" asked Alex.

"I don't know. Did you do what I did?"

"I don't know if you did what I did, but when I woke up this morning, I felt terrible, as if I was out all night long and I never had any sleep."

"This is weird, I feel the same and I had the strangest dream last night."

"I found this in my pocket this morning." Alex pulled out the pebble.

"So, it did happen."

"Did you get one too?"

Elsie pulled one out of her bag and they were identical. "So you were there with me last night?" asked Alex.

"Yeah, but Lilly, Josh and Juliana think they were somewhere else last night, but they were with us. I'm sure they were…, weren't they?"

"Yes, they were. Miss Borrow must have put some type of memory spell over them or something."

"What do you think happened to the crystals?"

"I don't know."

"What are they?" Juliana came from behind them and was looking at the pebbles.

"Ummm..., uh..., they are our pet rocks," said Alex, trying to make something up.

"Oh..., don't you think you guys are a bit old for pet rocks?"

"Not really," replied Elsie.

"Can you see what we wrote on them?" asked Alex.

Juliana looked closely at the pebbles, "No? I don't see any writing."

"Oh..., It must have rubbed off," said Elsie, looking at the pebbles. The school phoenix sang. It was time for class.

"We better go," said Alex.

Elsie went to pull out her timetable but decided not to. She knew exactly what was going to happen today. Classes would have changed now that Halloween holidays were coming up. There would be combined activities which included 'controlling your pet,' 'how to make your plants grow' and 'knowing your stars.' This was done before every school holiday because after the holidays were tests to see if you remembered what you had learnt.

Chapter 14. Classes

Elsie, Juliana and Alex walked out onto the school grounds. Everyone was there.

Grade ones were at the front right sitting on a big piece of tarp practising their ABC's with small words with bouncing letters made out of marshmallows floating around them. If they got one right, they could eat a letter. Alex wished he was in grade one.

The Grade twos were positioned to the front left of the field, identifying all floating shapes.

Grade threes were in the middle of the field on the right. They were jumping through floating hoops, crawling under chairs and jumping through skipping ropes.

Grade fours were in the middle on the left, making animated art out of paper, like walking paper people and animals. Most of them turned out extremely odd-looking.

Grade fives were at the back right-hand corner writing on floating Books.

The Grade sixes were up the back in the left corner, planting plants.

Last but not least was the Grade sevens, their grade. The whole class was right in the middle waiting for them to get there. She could see Josh standing right up the front waving to them. He looked so out of place.

"Class, my name is Mrs Fletcher. Your first lesson with me today will be Controlling Your Pet."

Mrs Fletcher knows all about animals. She has long wavy black hair, a large nose, long pointy fingers and always wears black and brown clothing. She looks a lot like a bird herself.

"Ok class, each of you will get an animal. I have cleared it with your parents and these animals will from now on be your pets. All animals have an animal instinct to go to the person whom it is drawn. No one is to move or call an animal to them. Just stand still and they will come to you. So here it goes."

Mrs Fletcher turned and opened a square wooden door on the ground. All kinds of animals came running out from underground to an owner. Lilly received a baby ball python. Juliana a frill neck lizard, Elsie a pink with black spots piglet and Josh received a Ferret.

"Aw…., why couldn't I get a black wolf, like Tim did? Instead, I get this smelly ferret," said Josh, picking his black and white ferret off the ground and looking at how straggly its fur was. Josh stared at a thin boy with his long black hair braided, patting his new grey wolf.

"Why didn't you get one Alex?" asked Juliana, looking over at Alex. He shrugged.

Mrs Fletcher looked at Alex with her big beady eyes then looked back at the door.

"It doesn't look like you are getting one," said Josh. Alex put his head down. He felt so embarrassed now that everyone was staring at him.

"Hey Alex, look," said Juliana. Alex put his head up and there was a black kitten with bright orange stripes and a bright red streak up the middle of its head, with its ears back running as fast as its little legs could run straight for Alex.

"wow!!!!!" said Josh.

Alex picked it straight up and hugged it.

"Cool," said Juliana.

"Nice kitty," said Lilly.

"Even a kitty like that I would have been happy with," replied Josh. Alex had a big smile on his face from ear to ear.

"Now class, since you all have your pets, it's time that we begin," said Mrs Fletcher.

The first task was 'teach your pet to stay'. Everyone put their pet away from them and had to get them to stay there. Elsie, Josh, Juliana, Lilly and Alex all tried to help each other.

Alex's kitten was doing very well. It tried to walk back to him twice, but the third time it stayed.

Juliana's pet lizard remained in the same spot the whole time like a statue except its tongue kept poking in and out, but other than that it was doing well.

Lilly's snake kept trying to climb up her leg and Josh's ferret kept bouncing, jumping and rolling. "Stop it, stop it. You're like a spring. Keep still," he was saying. Still, it kept jumping and running in circles. Everyone couldn't help but laugh. Josh stared at Tim again because his wolf was doing really good. "Aw why me?" said Josh. Mrs Fletcher was walking around the class with a clipboard marking how they were doing.

The next task was 'train your pet to jump'. Josh laughed. "This is going to be an easy one for me."

Everyone put their pets away from them again and said, "JUMP!"

Alex looked at his kitten and said, "I know you can do this." He smiled and said, "Jump." The kitten looked at him with puzzlement in its eyes.

"Like this," said Alex and jumped in the air. His kitten watched him and then tried to jump and fell over. Alex picked it up and patted it then put the kitten away from him.

"Try again... Jump." The kitten looked at him again and jumped. "Good boy." Alex looked over at Juliana's lizard. It was half way there, standing on its back legs.

Lilly looked like she was having a hard time. "Jump! I said Jump snake!" she went to pick the snake up and as soon as she touched the snake, it hissed at her and jumped nearly as high as her head. "Ah!" she yelled jumping backwards herself. Alex laughed and looked at Josh "Jump!!, Jump!!, Jump!! You stupid ferret! you were jumping before, now all you want to do is run in circles. Jump!!!" Josh was getting really cross. He bent down and said, "You are a stupid ferret. You never do what you are told to do and... and I don't want you!" The ferret looked up at Josh with big sad eyes like it was going to cry. A little tear fell down its cheek and its ears went down low.

"Look what you've done now! You don't deserve him. Do you know that? You really don't," said Elsie.

Josh looked at his ferret. "I'm so sorry I. I didn't mean it. I was just.... Oh, don't worry about me." He picked up the ferret. It curled itself up into Josh's arms. "It's not you. It's me." The ferret licked his face then ran back down to the ground.

"Can you jump for me please?" he asked. The ferret looked up at him and jumped into the air.

"Yes! he jumped!" The ferret climbed back up into his arms again. "Good boy Coco."

Tim looked over at him, laughed then bent down and patted his wolf.

"Don't worry about him," said Elsie.

"Well, he shouldn't stare at me like that. Or I might train Coco to bite his nose off," said Josh, now feeling quite proud of his ferret.

"Coco? I like it, suits him," said Alex.

"You four, stop talking. It's time for your pets to go back through the door until school has ended then you may have them back," said Mrs Fletcher, as she turned around to the door in the ground, opened it, blew a high pitch whistle and all the animals ran back through the door.

"Bye Coco! Look after yourself," said Josh, waving to his pet.

Once all the pets had gone inside Mrs Fletcher closed the door. "Time to swap positions with the grade six students. Miss Borrow will be your teacher so be on your best behaviour and show your manners at all times. Let's go, no fumbling," said Mrs Fletcher, leading them over to Miss Borrow.

"Good afternoon class. Today you will be learning how to grow your own tree. I know it may sound easy. Some of you may have grown a tree before. If not, you will learn something new and useful. Now everyone go and find a tree that attracts you," said Miss Borrow.

"Grow a tree. How can that be useful?" said Josh, looking at Lilly. Alex walked over to a spiky tree with orange coloured leaves. "You will do."

Lilly found herself a tree with baby blue flowers starting to grow on it.

Juliana walked up to several until she found one that she liked the most with all different colours. Josh found a tree that looked as though it was half asleep. Josh poked at the tree. "Ouch! What was that for?" It had spiked him, so he went looking for another tree finding one with green leaves. Josh touched one of the leaves "Ouch! Bloody hell why do they keep spiking me."

"I don't think they like you touching them," said Lilly, giggling. Finally, Josh found a short skinny tree with big orange leaves, "You will just have to do."

Miss Borrow walked to the front of the class, noticing that everyone had found themselves a tree. "I will give you a hint on how to make your trees grow, but you have to do most of it yourselves. Try and connect with your tree, be its friend, help it to trust you, try not to be too scared of it, don't hurt it or its feelings but don't be too soft on it either, they have to know who is boss. I will walk around the class and help anyone who is in need. You may start."

Alex looked at his tree from top to bottom, trying to figure out what to do. He saw the dirt gathered around the base of the tree, so he bent down to touch the soil.

"What do you think you are doing? Don't look at my roots! I'm not here for your amusement you know. Would you like it if I looked up your pants?" said a deep voice, coming from the tree. "Oh, sorry," said Alex, feeling embarrassed as he looked away and over to Lilly who was patting her tree saying, "You are a beautiful tree." Then she started to sing what sounded like a lullaby. The tree seemed to like what she was doing.

Alex looked back at his tree and said, "So…, do you want me to sing to you?" The tree sounded like it let out a laugh with its leaves rustling together. "I'm so very sorry dear boy I'm not like that. I prefer you know… Females… wood nymphs… I don't need you to serenade me."

"I…, I didn't mean it like that… Uhh… I'm so useless at this… Sooo…, How are you?"

"I was fine until you humans moved me here. I liked it where I was. I had friends there and now I am going to miss my weekly challenge of Guess The Breed."

"What type of Breeds?" asked Alex.

"Our breeds of course! Like the grumpy old oaks, gum trees, daffodils, palm trees, roses. The roses are so attractive you know. One grew right around me once. She was only attracted to me, being the youngest nicely trimmed tree that I was……, but then…, I went to sleep for a week or two and when I woke up, a new plant had moved in right next to me and she was all over him like a bee on pollen. I will never forgive her, and I will never go out with another rose again." The tree bent forward as if he put his head down, then straightened back up again, with his leaves all scrunched up like he was angry and said, "Why am I telling you this. You are only human. Go away. Leave me alone. I don't need someone listening to my life, especially a human…"

Alex thought about what Miss borrow had said 'be the boss'. "Well I didn't want to hear it anyway and you might like to know that I am a great player of Guess the Breed."

"Yeah right, how could a human, like you be good at a game we play?"

"Well you wouldn't know, would you? It's ok you are probably scared that I will win anyway." Alex turned away from the tree, as though he was going to walk away.

"No, wait! I am no scaredy-cat, I could beat you in a second."

"Yeah! You think so! Just try me," said Alex.

It worked. The tree and Alex started to play the game. Juliana looked like she was getting along with her tree too. They were both arm wrestling with each other and surprisingly the tree was winning, but Juliana kept on trying. She didn't want a tree to get the better of her.

Josh at first was trying to tell his tree to grow. "Grow! Grow!" "No! Make Me!" replied the tree, but after a while, he got sick of saying it and started to talk to it about what his dad did for a job. "That's great work, everyone. Your trees are looking good," said Miss Borrow.

"I win!" yelled Alex to his tree.

"How did you do it? How did you know so much?" asked the tree.

Miss Borrow said "Come over here everyone." Alex quickly looked back at the tree and said, "My mother worked at a florist." He walked away. He could hear the tree saying, "Damn it, I should have made an effort to know him first."

"I'm very proud of you. All your trees look great," said Miss Borrow. Alex looked back at his tree. It was giving him a dissatisfied look as though it wanted another game, but then he realised how much it had grown in that short amount of time.

"Wow, did I do that?" said Juliana, sounding very amazed and pleased with herself.

"Can I come back and see my tree?" asked Lilly.

"Any time you like. Listen up, everyone. Your next class is 'Know Your Stars' with Mr Orbissin. Follow me please."

Standing outside a small house the Year seven class waited patiently when the door started to open. "Good luck," said Miss Borrow and walked away.

The door opened. A man walked out, bending underneath the doorway. He was 6 feet 5 inches tall with short, thin blond hair, almost looking bald. He had the bluest eyes you've ever seen and wore big brown Boots, black shorts, and a black striped button-up shirt. Standing next to him was Lin. He stood the same height as Mr. Orbissins' knee.

"Come in, come in," said the little nerd in a squeaky voice. "Yes come in," said Mr Orbissin. He put his head down, put his shoulders forward and walked inside. The class followed him into the small house. It was dark. The floor was made out of light blue, glowing, coloured broken tiles that had been joined back together. The only light in the room was coming out of the roof where there was a large bright blue spiral staircase going up through the roof on the left side of the room. They followed Mr Orbissin up the stairs. It seemed to go on forever.

The walls around them had textured pastel blue and green striped wallpaper. Alex could see the tiny hole at the top of the stairs and the cone-shaped walls above him. As they walked higher, the walls looked like they were coming in on them, though they kept walking until they reached the top. Standing inside a giant see-through world globe, light beams were coming through the room in shades of blue, green and aqua. It was beautiful. There was a giant brown and black telescope in the middle of the room and there was a bench all the way around the walls, where they sat.

"This here is an astrological telescope," said Mr Orbissin, pointing at the telescope.

"But I am sure you all would know what it does." The class looked at him in a daze like they didn't have a clue.

"Oh really? What in Humbletin are they teaching you over there? Oh well, we better start right at the beginning then. Like I said before, this is an astrological telescope. You look through it and you can see anything you want to see in the universe. Some people have them built into their houses." Josh put his hand up in the air.

"Yes Josh?" asked Mr Orbissin.

"We have one in our house at home. My parents use it all the time."

"So, you would have a fair idea of how to use it?"

"Yes, Sir."

"Come up here then. You can show the class how you use it."

"Ok."

Josh stood up, walked over to the telescope and put his hand on a large handle and looked into the eyepiece.

Juliana looked at Elsie and whispered, "I can't wait for the holidays. I am going to yoga camp."

Mr Orbissin looked at them. "Oi! You two, you will be tested on this after the holidays, so I suggest you listen up." Mr Orbissin continued to point out all the parts of the telescope to the class.

"And Lilly's father is sending her away to The House of Etiquette."

Mr Orbissin turned his head around fast, glared at Juliana and Elsie. "Look here, if you two don't listen up, you can both leave my class."

"Sorry."

"Sorry," said Elsie and Juliana.

By the time class had finished, it was six o'clock at night. The school grounds were lit up. Alex, Elsie, Juliana, Lilly and Josh went to get their pets from Mrs Fletcher on the school grounds, but when they got there, everyone was gone. The door in the ground was locked.

"What do we do?" asked Lilly.

"Maybe we should go to Mrs Fletcher's classroom to see if she is there?" asked Alex.

"Wait, what's that?" asked Lilly, pointing over to a long van with bright-coloured flowers. Suddenly, the lights of the van flicked on and started to move slowly towards them.

"I don't know, but we are about to find out," replied Alex, walking backwards as it began moving faster like it was aiming to run over them. It stopped right in front of them. The side door slid open, out stepped a tall skinny man with long blond hair, a beard and moustache, wearing bright daggy multi-coloured clothing. "Dudes! What are you waiting for? I'm not going to wait out here all night. Come and get them." They walked over to the man as he pulled out a couple of big black boxes with handles. One of the boxes was nearly jumping out of the man's hands.

"Here you go, one for you Lilly, one for you Elsie, one for you Juliana and last but not least, one for you." he tried to hand Josh the big box that was jumping around, but it had jumped straight out of his hands and crashed onto the ground. Josh jumped backwards staring at the box. A little head poked out. "Coco! I'm so glad you're ok." The ferret ran up his leg and into his arms curling up into a ball.

Alex looked at the man wondering where his kitten was. "I'm so sorry, man... but... We couldn't find your kitten."

Alex put his head down. "I'm sorry Alex," said Elsie.

"It's alright... I suppose, I don't think I was meant to have a pet anyway," replied Alex, sadly with his head forward, Josh looked at the man with big eyes.

"Your...,"

"Mr Fletcher...,"

"I thought so," replied Josh.

"Well we better get going now," said Elsie.

"Good luck...," said Mr Fletcher, getting in his van then slowly driving away.

They all walked to the front gate together and said their goodbyes. "Goodbye Juliana. I will miss having you around," said Elsie.

"Don't worry I'll be back here in no time." Elsie nodded, gave her a hug and Julie walked off down the road. 'Boom, Boom, ting, ting, honk, honk!' Loud noises sounding like a drum, bell and a horn were coming down the road.

"What's that noise?" asked Alex.

"That's my dad." Lilly ran around and gave everyone a hug. Something that looked like a round bubble on wheels come around the corner. Boom, Boom, ting, ting, honk, honk.' They could see Lilly's father sitting up high in the bubble, almost like he was floating in the air. One side of the bubble began to slide down.

"Hello there, Elsie. Who is your friend?" asked the head, poking out with straight long pitch-black hair. "This is Alex."

"Hi there Alex. I'm Mr Drahon, Lilly's father."

"Nice to meet you, Sir," replied Alex. Mr Drahon stepped out of the bubble, leaving one foot inside. The bubble began to shrink and change form quickly. It shrunk that much that there was nothing left but a blue shoe on Mr Drahons' foot which looked rather odd with his black trench coat and long black pants.

"Well we must go now Lilly. Say your goodbyes," said Mr Drahon. "Bye everyone. Hope to see you soon." Lilly waved.

Mr Drahon bowed and put his foot out. The Boot began to grow more significant into the shape of a bubble again. Lilly and her father climbed into the bubble. You could see them floating up into the middle. "See you two later then," said Josh, as he waved and walked off quickly.

Chapter 15. Surprise

When Alex and Elsie arrived home, there was a light shining through the lounge room window. They could hear Mr and Mrs McKormick talking out loud. "Listen to me, Hazel, the girl, knows best."

"She is too young to decide."

"She is of age."

"She can't go, she just can't go!"

"Yes, she can!"

Alex and Elsie peeked through a gap in the window.

"Look, Hazel," said Frank, holding Hazel's chin, looking into her eyes and continues to say, "The girl has to make up her own mind. If that's what she wants to do then let her. You have to stop the modcoddling. She knows what she is doing." Elsie could hear her mother crying.

"It's ok..., everything will work out," said Frank, with his arms around Hazel. "But, how, how do you know?"

"That's it, I'm going in," said Elsie, walking up to the front door and opening it. "Elsie! Alex!" said her father, startled.

Hazel turned from them and wiped her eyes so they couldn't see she had been crying.

"Mum why are you crying?" asked Elsie, holding the box with her pet piglet inside.

"Sweetie now that you have your new pet, we had to give Boots away. I have been so worried about telling you. We can't afford to keep them both."

"But mum."

"Yes, I know you loved him, but he has gone to a good home and the nice lady who has him said that you could visit him any time you like."

Elsie looked at her with sad eyes. She loved her cat Pussin Boo. "And darling we have some more news for you," said her father.

"When we gave Boots away to this nice lady, we found out that you know her very well."

"I do?" asked Elsie.

"Her name is Miss Borrow," said her mum.

Elsie put her head down, trying not to make eye contact with her parents. Mr McKormick walked up to Elsie put his hand under her chin, lifted her head back up and said, "Yes we know darling, news travels fast in Humbletin, but you shouldn't be ashamed of it. A lot of people are interested in herbs and plants."

"Pardon?" asked Elsie.

"Miss Borrow has been teaching you both about plants, hasn't she?" asked Mrs McKormick.

"Uh, yes, yes she has?"

Mr McKormick gave her a wink. "So you've got your old father's interests, have ya? That's great darling. I knew Miss Borrow when I was a child and that's how I know everything I know now." Mrs McKormick rolled her eyes as to say… 'here he goes again.' Elsie took her new pet piglet out of the box and showed her parents.

"Aw…. isn't he just lovely Frank?" said Mrs McKormick. "He is going to love it in his new pen we have made for him outside."

"I hope so," replied Elsie.

"Why don't you take him outside and wash your hands for dinner sweetie."

"Ok mum," said Elsie, as she walked outside.

"So Alex, where is your new pet?"

"I think they lost him," Alex replied sadly.

"Awe that's no good deary. I'm sure he will turn up somewhere."

That night, Elsie was lying in bed when there was a knock at the door.

"It's me, sweetie, can I come in for a minute?"

"Just a second father," she replied.

Elsie put her baby blue robe over her white satin nightdress, then opened the door for her father to come in. "I have something to tell you, Elsie."

"What is it, father? Nothing has happened to any of our cousins, has it? Not little Janny is it? I haven't seen little Janny for a while."

"No, no, no there is nothing wrong. If you like I can get Aunt Shirley to drop little Janice off one day and you can look after her for the day."

"Yes please, it would be nice to see little Jan Jan."

Her father sat on the chair in the room and Elsie sat on the side of her bed.

"The reason why I came to see you is to talk about Miss Borrow."

"What did she say, dad? I didn't mean to go there. I just wanted to have fun with my friends. I know it's off limits but...,"

"I am not getting mad at you Elsie. I wanted to tell you that Miss Borrow did teach me a lot of different things and... there is something else, I have to ask you."

"What is it, father?"

"Did Miss Borrow show you something, something special, like a doorway?"

"Well, umm."

"It's ok you can tell me."

"I guess you could call it a door...,"

"And what did this doorway look like?"

He leaned forward on the chair looking quite intense.

"Well…., it looks…, something…., like……, it's hard to explain. Why do you want to know?"

"Come on! Just tell me."

Elsie felt her father was acting very irregularly. She had never seen her father this interested in anything before. "There were vines."

"I knew it. It really is it, isn't it?"

"What do you mean?"

Her father moved forward more on the chair and whispered in a deep voice that sent chills down Elsie's spine. "Fabilchi."

"Yes." She breathed out the word like she was admitting that she had committed a crime. Her father sat back on his seat realising that he was starting to scare Elsie and said, "It's ok love, I just wanted to let you know that I also went to Fabilchi when I was young, and I was just wondering if it was still there and if it looked the same is all. Nothing to worry about. Mother doesn't know about it, well, being such a mysterious place that had to be kept a secret. She only knows that Miss Borrow taught about plants there. Well, we will talk another time, into bed now." He gave her a kiss on her forehead, and she slid into bed.

That night Alex laid in bed rolling the object that his father had given to him in his hands back and forth, thinking of

Elsie and her parents. 'Knock, knock, knock.' There was a knock coming from the bedroom window. Alex looked quickly. There was a tree outside, and a kitten was sitting on the branch with its tail swaying from side to side. He jumped up out of bed. He ran over to the window, noticing it was the kitten from school. The kitten purred with big wide eyes. He looked at Alex and his mouth opened, "Alex!"

"You can speak?"

The kitten spoke quickly, "Yes, I am from Fabilchi. I'm sorry I could not tell you today, but I couldn't risk being heard by everyone there. I have to go now. I was sent to tell you that there is trouble in Fabilchi. We need you there right now a.s.a.p. Goodbye Alex," and the kitten vanished. Alex stood there scratching his head not knowing what to do. 'I better tell Elsie,' He said to himself, as he moved to the door and put his hand on the doorknob to open it. "What do you think you're doing?" Alex was startled from the deep groaning voice.

"Who's there," Alex whispered softly looking around the room. "Get your hand off me and I will tell you," It said in a very slow deep voice. Alex looked down at his hand and let go of the round doorknob. As he looked closer there was a pair of eyes between the long cracks in the door. 'Cough,' 'cough,' 'cough,' dust came shooting out of a small gap beneath the handle.

"As I said before... what do you think you are doing Alex?"

"Uhh..., Well...,"

"I was warned about you," said the door, blinking and looking at him rather curiously.

"Warned? What do you mean?"

"I was told to keep an eye on you, just in case you go wondering around where you shouldn't go."

"I'm not going to roam around."

"Then what in heaven's name are you doing then?"

"I'm... well... I Just... I am just going to get a drink is all... I'm allowed to be thirsty, aren't I?"

"I didn't say you were not allowed. However, it is my job to make sure you do not get into any trouble while you are here, after all, I was sleeping." The door yawned that large Alex could see straight through to the other side. It slowly opened with a deep groan as the eyes and mouth disappeared. Alex took a step out of the room trying hard not to make any noise 'creak...' The sound of a floorboard creaked as he put his foot down. "Shh… please...," he whispered to the floorboard as it moved a little then straightened out.

'They were not kidding about things being alive,' Alex continued to say under his voice. Alex walked along in the pitch dark with his arms out in front of him trying to feel his way around.

"Hey," a deep voice thundered right next to Alex. "Who are you?" he asked. "Who are you?"

"I asked you first."

"I asked you second."

"Is that you, Brandon?"

"Is that you, Theodore?"

"Uh...," Alex turned around and bumped straight into Mr McCormick. "Oh, it's you, Alex, what are you doing?"

"Uh..., I was thirsty."

"Oh right...,"

"What were you doing?"

"Uh..., I was thirsty too."

"Um ok...,"

"Where are we? Let me turn on the light."

Frank turned on the light and they were both standing near the front door. "Ok, let's get a drink, then off to bed."

The next morning Alex woke up to the sounds of yelling and screaming. "I DON'T WANT TO GO! YOU CAN'T MAKE ME!"

"Oh yes, I can son."

"Nooooo Not the soap!!!!"

"You better get up there and get dressed, or this soap will be in your mouth, boy!"

Alex heard thundering thuds going up the stairs. He figured it was Brandon. "Morning," said Alex, as he walked out into the dining room. "Quick Alex here."

Hazel pointed to toast waiting for him on the table.

"Eat that up, then go and get dressed in these." She then pointed to a beautiful, silky, purple long-sleeved button top and a pair of long black pants that were hanging over one of the chairs.

"Oh, and here take this as well deary." She picked up a black-tie from the bench and put it on the other pieces of clothing.

"We are all going to get our portraits taken today, so everyone has to look their very best."

When everyone was ready and standing out the front yard, they all squashed into the patchwork automobile and when Mr McKormick started it up, Alex could hear the gears inside the automobile crunching and straining. It started to move, and they headed off up a winding road to a large house on top of the hill. Mr McKormick stepped out of the automobile, straightened up his clothes then said, "Come on you lot, let's get a move on. Henry hasn't got all day. His work is so good. He is in demand you know."

"Yes, move on children," said Mrs McKormick, as they all piled out of the automobile.

Spitting on her hand and smoothing down Brandon's hair. "Oh Mum," said Brandon, pushing her hand aside as they walked up the path.

Mr McKormick took hold of the heavy brass door knocker, shaped like a huge paintbrush, and banged it slowly onto the brass plate attached to the solid wooden door.

The door opened. A man walked out with a strange-shaped wooden contraption strapped to his waist. It had ten long wooden arms coming off of it holding paintbrushes. Mr McKormick attempted to flatten his hair down with his hand and said, "Everyone this is Henry, the portrait painter."

"Nice to meet you," said Henry, trying to bow but only being able to lean forward a little.

"You too," said Mrs McKormick.

"Come in, come in."Everyone walked into the house one by one. "Mind the mess."

"I'm not minding it, you mind it, Elsie," said Brandon.

"What?"

"No, no, I mean…., Uhh… don't worry about it, come in," said Henry.

"Ok, that's enough of that children," replied Mr McKormick, giving Elsie and Brandon a stern look.

"Walk this way," said Henry.

He led them to a vast room empty except for a large uniquely carved wooden chair and a big heap of glowing orbs lying on the ground.

"Now, Mr McKormick, what type of portraits would you like today?" asked Henry.

"One of all the family this time thanks, Henry."

"Ok then, what type of background would you like?"

"Hmm…, how about…," Mr McKormick gazes into the air then slightly jumps as he comes up with an idea. "Our home?"

"No problem."

"I will just have to get an image of it." He clicked his fingers three times, then three more times. They watched, the big heap of glowing orbs lift high up into the air and right out of the window.

"What are they doing?" asked Elsie, as the orbs vanished out of view.

"Won't take a second," and then the orbs flew straight back through the window and splattered against the big blank wall creating an identical image of the McKormick's house.

"Cool!!" said Brandon, starring at the wall with his mouth wide open.

"You think that's cool watch this," said Henry.

Henry quickly clicked his fingers twice, then twice again then suddenly out of two other cluttered rooms in the house, came a workbench, a saw, a hammer, nails and then what seemed to be a little round light. Dust was flying everywhere. No one could see anything, then the dust cleared, and the small round light flew fast out of the room. Left standing in the room were five new wooden chairs.

"That's......, Awesome...," Brandon's mouth was now that wide you would think it was touching the floor.

"Sure is, now go sit and I'll paint your portrait."

Henry clicked his fingers again but this time in a rhythm. Out came his easel with a piece of white fabric on it.

"Ok sit still," said Henry and all of his brushes started to paint on a square piece of silky, white cloth. "Ok done, have a look," said Henry.

The McKormick's walked over to the piece of fabric. "Oh my, goodness," said Mrs McKormick.

"Wow," said Elsie.

"It looks like an identical picture of us," said Mr McKormick. Henry clicked twice and clicked a fast click twice again.

The little round light returned, and collected the fabric from Henry, then suddenly the workbench and tools appeared again same as before they went to work finishing the picture off by framing it. The glowing light collected the magnificent portrait, all framed, flew through the air and lightly placed it in Henry's hands.

"Here you go Elsie, you can hold onto it," said Henry.

The little glowing light went up to Henry's ear and then sat on his shoulder. "Oh, I am terribly sorry. I forgot to introduce you to my important business partner. His name is Zaby, my carpenter."

The Mckormicks looked really closely and they could see a little gold mist-like orb with a little man inside it sitting on Henry's shoulder.

"Hello friends. I am Zaby, nice to meet you," he said in a little voice then stood up on Henry's shoulder and nearly fell over. He put his little hand out to shake theirs. Mr McKormick put his hand out and Zaby shook the tip of his finger. "Nice to meet you too."

They heard a knocking at the door.

"More folks are wanting a portrait. It's never-ending."

"Well, I suppose we had better get a move on." Mr McKormick paid Henry.

"Thank you all for coming. It has been a pleasure," said Henry.

"Thank you," said Mrs McKormick.

They all walked back outside one by one, then hurdled into the automobile, waving to Henry and Zaby, and then set off back home.

Later that evening, Alex was lounging on his bed looking at the orb when he heard a knock at the front door and Elsie yelling out, "I'll get it mum!" He could hear her running down the stairs. "Oh MY!" Alex heard Elsie yell, so he jumped up out of bed and ran out to see what it was.

Alex noticed that there were two tables, each filled with a variety of foods: Apricot Bomb Tumblers (they spin and jump around when you pour them into a bowl of milk), Tuning Cheese Bubblers (Long tubes made out of cheese in shapes of whistles. When you dip them in a cheesy dip you can blow bubbles that make sounds), Tornado Twisted Twiggys (spinning around on the table like small tornadoes), Flaming Fury Volcanos (toast with sweet chilly and cheese that form a volcano, Elsie's favourite), Flying Snow Snaps (Thin, sweet coconut deserts that fly around the room and snap at you if you try to catch them. The only way to eat them is to catch them with your mouth).

Sitting at each end of the table were her Mother and Father. "Where is your brother, Elsie? He should be awake by now," asked her father, as Elsie went and answered the door.

"Surprise!!!" Standing there were all her friends and Miss Borrow. Elsie didn't know what to do.

"Hey Elsie," said Juliana, with a smile.

"Well, are you going to let us in or not?" asked Josh, with a grin. Elsie led them into the dining room.

"Your mum told us about you and Alex being accepted to do Flora Philosophy with Miss Borrow, (Miss Borrow smiled at them) and invited us over for a gathering."

"Have a seat, everyone. There is more than enough room," said Hazel. Everyone sat at the table. Alex was feeling extremely confused about everything and then a thought struck him, will Miss Borrow get mad at him for not turning up in Fabilchi last night? He had forgotten all about it until now. He looked over at Elsie who seemed to be having the best time laughing with her friends. After everyone finished eating except for Brandon of course, they went out into the backyard to play a few games, such as find the pixie and count the moles.

Alex had to leave halfway through the game Hunt the Hamster to go to the bathroom, when walking up the hallway he bumped into someone.

"Oh sorry, I seem to be bumping into everyone lately," said Alex, as he looked up at Miss Borrow.

"That's ok Alex. How do you like the gathering?"

"It's excellent. I'm glad you are all here for Elsie."

"We are not just here for Elsie, we are also here for you and since the time is now…," Miss Borrow stopped talking and looked up to the shadow on the roof, then continued to say, "4pm you and Elsie should start getting ready soon."

"For what?"

"Your lessons, of course."

"Lessons? I didn't know, I thought…,"

"Well now you do." smiled Miss Borrow.

"Ok, I'll just go and tell Elsie."

"No need to sweetie. She is already on her way inside right about…," They looked behind them as Elsie walked through the back door. "…Now," finished Miss Borrow.

"Ha!" laughed Alex.

"See you soon Alex and you too Elsie! Nice gathering, I loved it!"

"Well… we better get ready then, see you soon."

Alex turned around to go to the bathroom and then turned back to wave goodbye to Miss Borrow, but she was nowhere to be seen.

Chapter 16. Sail Away

Alex and Elsie walked through the hedges at the back of Elsie's yard.

"Why couldn't we have just used the pebbles," asked Alex.

"I want to see what it's like this way, I've been living here my entire life and it never even crossed my mind to look beyond the hedges."

"Obviously Brandon did."

"Yeah well, he is just a mischief-maker. Couldn't you tell by the way those gnomes were looking at us?"

"I suppose they did seem a bit wary of us," replied Alex, as they walked along the pathway next to the mist,

"Is it just me, or does it seem a bit spookier this time of day?" asked Elsie.

"It is getting a wee bit dark."

All of a sudden, a gust of wind came, pushing them forward along the pathway, then settle down into a gentle breeze. "What was that?" asked Elsie.

"I don't know. Is someone there!?" Alex yelled out.

Then another more significant wind pushed them forward, almost knocking them over. It stopped. "Listen," said Alex.

"What? I can't hear anything."

"Shh, just listen."

Elsie heard a soft whisper on the air. "It sounds like my name."

"I thought it sounded like my name." Then the sound started getting louder.

"No, it, it sounds like chanting," said Alex, as he walked closer to the mist. "It's coming from the mist," he said, as he started to put his ear against the mist.

"NOOO! DON'T DO THAT ALEX!"

Alex didn't take any notice and put his ear against the mist, then jumped backwards clutching at his ear. "AHH!"

"What is it? What happened?" asked Elsie.

"LOUD!" he yelled.

"Loud?"

"Yeah!"

As Elsie was looking at Alex, she noticed a HUGE shadow coming towards them through the mist.

"OH My…," she said, looking at the shadow, then looking at Alex standing right beside it.

"You might want to move," said Elsie, with wide eyes looking at the mist.

Alex looked at the mist and noticed the Huge shadow and moved slowly back towards Elsie. "What? What is it?" asked Alex.

"I... I don't know. It's not chanting it' s.., singing and..., I... I know that voice. I've heard it before."

"I think I can see it. It's getting clearer," said Alex.

"The words, I've heard them be.... Be.... Before." The words stumbled out of Elsie's mouth as she looked at the now fully formed Spanish galleon, the biggest ship she had ever seen, as it began to appear right in front of her eyes.

The deep voices were making the ground vibrate underneath their feet.

Sail away me matey, Sail away with me,

Sail away me matey, Take me to the sea,

Mye heart lives for, Nowhere onshore,

But on the deep blue sea,

Bring up the anchor, Scrub down the deck,

Give me some money or Even a cheque, But

Sail away me matey, for life on the sea is for me,

Sail away me matey, give me, me ship and I am free!

Alex looked at Elsie. Her eyes were wide open, and she was as white as a ghost.

"Mr Bucklesworth." He heard her say under her breath, then he looked up to where she was looking and noticed someone leaning over the side of the ship looking at him. "Good day me mateys," the man called out.

"Mr Bucklesworth!" Elsie yelled out loud.

"Aye, Aye, it is me, Mr Bucklesworth!" he said, stretching his arms out wide. The large baggy sleeves of his brown pirate shirt dangled off his arms. His long wavy hair was blowing back from all the wind in the mist. "Oops," he said, as he just caught his large black pirate hat that had almost fallen off of his head. "Would ya like to jump aboard an sail with me mates and Aye? We can drop ya off wherever ya headin. Me ship sails the mist as straight and sharp as a Captain's sword and as fast as a monkey with its bum on fire." Alex and Elsie laughed as they watched a long rope ladder descend down towards them. They climbed up the ladder and onto the ship.

"I didn't know you had a ship, Mr Bucklesworth," said Elsie.

"Shh....!! Don't let them catch you calling me that," he said, as he pointed into the distance. Alex looked at where he was pointing. He could see a group of huge, muscled men, but the longer Alex looked at them, the more he could see that they were not men at all, but looked like they were made from something else altogether.

"They remind me of something," he said out loud to himself.

"Elementals," said Elsie.

Alex then realised they reminded him of the mysterious orb that his father had given him.

"You can't call me that, on this ship. My name is Captain Blackbird. If they hear you calling me anything else… you don't want to know. Anyway, where are ya heading to?"

A big, sleek black crow flew across the sky and landed on his shoulder. He pointed at the crow, "Oh and by the way, this is me lifelong friend, the Immortal Morrigan. She has been with me all of me life."

The crow put her head up. Her eyes were a dark red. The Captain whistled two high pitch notes. The giant red, white, brown and blue Elementals that were standing in a group started walking over, their feet thumping. Alex observed with keen interest that the red elementals before him were not completely solid; instead, they shimmered with a delicate transparency. Flickering tongues of flame danced within their forms, giving them a mesmerizing quality as they swirled and glowed like living embers, their fiery essence casting an enchanting warmth in the air around them.

A massive boulder resting on the deck began to tremble, cracks spidering across its surface as it undulated with a life of its own. Gradually, the rock reshaped itself, muscles and features emerging, until it took on the unmistakable form of a man. Alex's eyes widened in astonishment as he scanned the ship, realizing that other large boulders scattered around were also stirring, their rugged surfaces shifting and morphing, each one beginning its own transformation into humanoid figures. The air was thick with a sense of magic and mystery as the once-static stones came alive in a breathtaking display.

As he scanned the eerie landscape, his gaze was drawn to wispy, ethereal figures emerging from the swirling mist that enveloped the ship. These ghostly apparitions ebbed and flowed like smoke, their forms twisting and coiling as they danced in the damp air. Meanwhile, a steady stream of water gushed forth from large, wooden barrels, cascading down onto the deck and began to coalesce, taking shape and transforming into towering, humanoid figures—massive beings that loomed larger than life, their features obscured by the swirling fog.

"Alex, Elsie, this is me crew, The Elemental Resilients, meaning the hard-wearing men that never die." Elsie stepped backwards afraid that she was going to be knocked over. They heard a voice yelling out, "Let me go! Let me go! or I'll put your lights out!"

Then a deep voice yelled out that made the deck of the ship vibrate. "CAPTAIN! HE HAS DONE IT AGAIN!' A Fire Elemental came forward through the others and it was holding Josh upside down by his foot. "Put me down! Captain! Tell inferno to put me down! INFERNO! PUT ME DOWN!" Captain Blackbird looked at the Fire Elemental. His face was making different expressions as if he was talking to the captain, although his mouth never opened. The elemental dropped Josh onto the deck of the ship.

"Oww! What did you drop me for?!" yelled Josh, his slightly red cranky face looking up at the Fire Elemental.

The Captain looked at Josh and said quickly, "What were you doing down in the ship's cellar again boy?"

"Well, I, ah, I saw something shiny and I wondered what it was," said Josh. "You are too sticky boy. One of these days that stickybeak of yours is going to get you in big, big trouble. Get back to work, up the sails."

"Yes, Captain."

Elsie looked at the Captain with a worried look on her face.

"Don't worry little miss, you haven't done anything against our crew, yet.." said the Captain.

"What did he do?" asked Alex.

"A long time ago, we found this boy inside our ships cellar. We had guessed that he was four years old. However, he was extremely clever for his age and it looked like he knew exactly what he was doing. We caught him with his pockets full of our treasures. We thought that someone had put him up to it, so we tried to find his parents and well, he ended up getting adopted by a scientist because we could not find his parents. He kept saying to us over and over again some strange names that we had never heard before and insisted that one of our treasures was his. I can remember it like it was yesterday. It was a pocket watch, carved with dragons and some sort of runes on it. We have caught him in there a few times since then. We think he might be trying to look for it. The strangest thing is, it's been missing ever since that day."

"Umm...," said Alex, in a bit of shock, as he was thinking back to the day that he had given a man in a boat the exact thing the Captain was talking about. He continued, "What, uh, do you remember at all, what the names were?" The Captain looked at him in puzzlement. "Well... It was a long time ago. I think it was something like, I inland, uh..., Henge, uh... It was just garbled words. We really couldn't make any sense of the words at all, oh... And Dubin."

Alex couldn't believe what he was hearing. He didn't know what to make of it all.

"Ok well, enough chinwagging. It's time to sail. Where does your destiny lie?"

"Rottingwood," said Elsie, looking at Alex with a worried expression on her face.

"Ah...., The Mistress herself, to The Mistress me crew! set sail!"

'Thump, Thump, Thump Thump,' the crew started to stamp their feet while working on the ship and the Captain began to sing the ship's song to the beat of the crew.

Sail away me matey, Sail away with me,

Sail away me matey, Take me to the sea,

Me heart lives for Nowhere onshore,

But on the deep blue sea,

Bring up the anchor, Scrub down the deck,

Give me some money or Even a cheque, But

Sail away me matey, For life on the sea is for me,

Sail away me matey, Give me, me ship and I am free!

"LAND HO!" yelled Josh at the top of the sail post.

"We are here already?" asked Alex, as he walked to the side of the ship and looked overboard. He could see the roof of Rottingwood, a loud horn bellowed. Alex looked up at Josh who was holding a big cone-shaped, shell horn and was blowing into it, his face going red.

Then a grinding sound came from beneath them. He looked back over the side of the ship and could see the roof tiles of Rottingwood sliding aside creating a large round opening. The rope ladder was flung overboard down into the opening in the top of the roof.

"Good Luck Me Matey's!" said the Captain, as Alex and Elsie turned around to climb over the side of the ship.

"Good Luck!" they heard a female voice say, they turned back around to see who had said it, when they saw a beautiful pale woman with long black wavy hair standing next to the Captain, she was wearing a long black dress made out of feathers and on her back was a broad set of black feathered wings. She was holding onto the Captain's hand.

"Uh, thanks..., Lady Morrigan," replied Alex, as he started to climb over the side of the ship.

Alex was holding onto the bottom of the ladder with Elsie above him. "What do I do now?" he yelled.

"Let Go!" shouted the Captain over the side of the ship.

"Let Go?!?!" yelled Alex.

"YES! LET GO!" yelled the Captain.

Alex let go and vanished down into the building. All went black.

Chapter 17. Keeper

Alex looked downwards while falling into the darkness. There was a blue light and as he got closer, it was getting brighter and brighter, until all around him was blue. Feeling he was no longer falling, but floating slowly, he looked upwards and could see Elsie coming down. "Elsie!"

"Alex?" she replied.

Alex flapped his arms up and down and he found he could make himself go even slower. Elsie was getting closer and closer until she was right beside him.

"Elsie."

"Alex."

"What's happening?"

"I don't know, I've never, ever, experienced anything like this." Alex looked down again and could now see green and small shapes.

"I don't know, but I think we are about to find out," said Alex, pointing downwards.

As they got closer to the ground, the shapes started to take form and they could see people walking around.

"Fabilchi!" they yelled, not realising how loud they were until their voices echoed around Fabilchi. Floating downwards, they saw everyone and everything staring at them.

"Sorry."

"Sorry."

Miss Borrow walked up to them looking serious.

"Sorry, Miss, we didn't realise how loud we…,"

Miss Borrow cut him off in mid-sentence, "Not now, we have more important matters to address. The Simulcast is loose in Fabilchi and we need your help. When you came through the hedge on Halloween night, you brought it with you. Did you encounter any unusual happenings the other night once you went through the hedge?"

"Uh…," said Alex, not knowing what to say because everything that had happened since he had been here, he would class as unusual.

"Yes," said Elsie.

"And what was it? What happened?"

"Juliana had Sim and she was almost pulled down into a hole in the ground. All of these hands were trying to…," Miss Borrow cut her off, "Yes…, yes…, that was the Souls of Hells Gates." Alex looked at her with an open mouth. "Yes Alex, they are very dangerous. I can't even begin to think of how you all escaped. No one has ever." She stopped and rubbed the back of her neck with her right hand then continued, "Well it's too late now. I would have thought that the souls of the dead might have taken the Simulcast.

However, there have been recent events that tell us otherwise. This is why I sent for you the other night Alex, but all that doesn't matter now. What matters the most is that you are here."

"What do we need to do?" asked Alex.

"There lies the problem. Usually, when a Simulcast is released into the world, there is nothing that can be done."

Alex and Elsie looked at each other than Miss Borrow continued, "However, I have been contacted by Gia and she tells me there is a way."

"There is? What do we do?" asked Elsie.

"Well, I'm sorry to have to say this Elsie, but this is one event you will need to stay out of. However, we will have other things that you will need to do, but we will get back to that soon. There is an ancient fable that has been passed down through the centuries, not many people remember it. It's of a boy who had come from a different time and a different dimension. They called him The Keeper."

"The Keeper? Where can we find this boy?" asked Alex.

"He is standing right in front of me," replied Miss Borrow. Alex stared at Miss Borrow trying to comprehend what she had just said.

"What? Me?" he replied.

"Yes, you."

"But I'm just, Keeper? Keeper of what?"

"I think you know of what Alex." Alex stood there thinking, "But I don't own anything."

"Don't you?"

Alex thought some more and just then, he realised precisely what Miss Borrow was talking about.

"But I, I can't. It's my Father's. If he knew, if he found out." Miss Borrow just kept looking at him.

"What? What is it? Alex?" asked Elsie.

"It's, it's, I'm not allowed," he said, then thought to himself, how would my father find out anyway? After all, he is in a totally different place now.

"Ok…, It's a, an orb."

"An orb? What does it look like?" asked Elsie.

"It's really hard to explain."

"Then why don't you show it to her, Alex?" asked Miss Borrow.

"Show her? How?"

"This is Fabilchi, isn't it?"

"Yeah?"

"Anything you think of in here happens, so if you think of the orb."

The next second Alex held out his hand, a mist twirled within it and the orb appeared.

"Wow," said Elsie.

"It's working!" announced Alex as he held his hand out for everyone to see the orb and its colourful bouncing balls and cogs inside.

"Can I hold it?" asked Elsie.

"Sure."

As soon as Alex put the orb into Elsie's hand, it stopped glowing.

"What happened?"

"It only works when Alex holds it. It is in tune with his aura," said Miss Borrow.

"His Aura?" asked Elsie.

"Yes, his aura. This is one of the things you will be learning here with me. We have a lot to work on. You will both be staying here with me for a while. Your parents know Elsie, and all of your luggage is already here for both of you. Come this way." They walked across the green land and to a forest area. Little men and little women were walking around with bright red hair and long beards.

"This is where we will be staying."

"We?" asked Elsie.

"Yes, I will be staying here with you. I have a house of my own over here." She pointed to a large tree with windows and a door. Alex looked around and saw that most of the houses within the trees had small doors and windows. "This is where the dwarves live, and you must always treat them with respect. This is their home, and this will be your home for now." Miss Borrow pointed to a tree that was just beside hers.

"I will let you both go and get your things sorted. Come and see me when you are all settled in."

"Ok."

"Ok Miss Borrow."

When Alex looked around, lanterns were hanging around the trees, beautiful soft light shining through the branches here and there.

He could hear the soft wind blowing through the trees, the occasional sound of wind chimes, little children giggling and playing, and the smell of cedar wood wafted under Alex's nose. He took a deep breath in, then let it out slowly, everything was so green and beautiful.

"Are you coming in or not?" asked Elsie, as her head peeked around the corner of the door.

"I'm coming," he replied, walking into the tree house.

Inside the tree house were vines covering the walls. There was no roof. It was almost like the whole tree was hollow. Steps were coming from out of the walls leading up in a spiral. Floating egg-shaped chairs that looked like they were made from transparent green leaves and little yellow lights were floating around in the air.

"Well, I guess our bedrooms are up there?" asked Alex.

"I really hope we don't have to climb all those stairs."

"Me to, maybe we should go and ask?

"Yes, let's do that."

Alex led the way outside and to the door of Miss Borrows house and knocked.

"Come in!" They heard her shout.

Alex opened the door and they walked inside. This house looked the same as their tree house.

"Uh, Miss Borrow, how do we get to our bedrooms?" asked Elsie. "Well like this of course." She walked over to one of the egg chairs and sat in it.

"You just have to think of where you want to be and...,"

All of a sudden, the chair began to float upwards. They could hear Miss Borrow yelling, "Go, try it!"

Alex led the way outside and back to their own place. "Ok, here goes nothing," said Elsie, sitting in a chair, then floating upwards until she vanished from sight. Alex sat in a chair and thought 'my room, my room.' He started to rise up and up until he could see tunnels surrounding him. He floated towards one of the tunnels, then into the tunnel. He could now see a large room, bright with light. The chair floated downwards into the room and settled with Alex's feet just touching the ground. He stood up and noticed his bag that Elsie's parents had given him on top of a wooden bed with a latticework canopy, dark green pillow slips and a dark green blanket. "Wow, somehow I still feel like I am dreaming."

Chapter 18. The Shadow

When Alex and Elsie went back to see Miss Borrow, they found her waiting. "Did you bring your crystals?" she asked.

"Yes."

"Yes."

"That's good. Elsie, you can go with Alex on one condition."

"Ok."

"You cannot go anywhere near where Alex is from."

Elsie nodded.

"Ok then, now all you have to do is think of the name of the person you want to see while you are holding the crystal and you will appear at your destination.

"Who do we see again?" asked Elsie.

"Her name is Gia, Goddess of the earth."

"Ok and what do we do when we get there?"

"Gia will explain everything. Now hold onto your crystals and think of where you want to be."

Alex and Elsie held their crystals tightly. A mist began to develop around them. Alex felt his pocket getting warm and vibrating. Realising that the orb was still there, he put his hand into his pocket and held the orb. The crystals started to change colour from brown, white, red then blue. The mist began to clear, and they were in the middle of a rainforest.

"Are we here?" asked Elsie.

"I guess so," Alex replied, as he took his hand back out of his pocket, looked around and continued to say, "I wonder where she is. I'm guessing that she can't be too far away."

"I hope not. I would hate to be lost here."

"Don't worry, we will be fine."

Elsie gasped in surprise. Alex looked at her and noticed that she was looking behind him. Alex turned around. "What?" he asked.

"Look, can't you see her?"

Alex looked at the green leaves and bushes and then, he noticed a green, womanly, shaped figure in between the trees. She blended in like she was part of the nature that surrounded her. "Um..., hi, Gia?" asked Alex. The lady nodded slowly.

"Miss Borrow said that you were expecting us."

She nodded again and then pointed to a long log lying on the ground.

"You want us to sit down?" asked Elsie. The lady nodded again.

Alex and Elsie sat on the log. Alex opened his mouth to speak, but then he noticed he was feeling very drowsy and tired. He was finding it hard to keep his eyes open. Slowly, he began to slant sideways and then was lying on his side on the log. "What's happening?" he asked softly. He heard a small voice say, "I found him, Master. I found him." Alex managed to open his eyes a little and could see a small gnome that looked just like Sim. He was looking up at an enormous red beast. The beast's long snout with rows of sharp teeth opened wide and let out a deep growl then began to speak, "Why didn't you get it? You are useless. You could have at least brought the twins? Instead, you come to me with nothing."

"But I brought news, Master and I will get them. I promise you."

"Don't go making promises that you will not keep, or I will make sure that you will suffer. Painfully……,"

"Yes, yes Master," said the Simulcast, starting to tremble.

"Now GO! GO gather the rest. Find the twins and bring them to me!"

Alex blinked and everything went blurry. He blinked again and they were gone. He could see Elsie lying on the ground near where Gia was standing, with the bright green grass around her. He sat up and looked around. Gia was gone.

"Elsie…, Elsie?" he said quietly. He stood up then went and kneeled on the ground next to her.

"Elsie?" He put his hand on her arm. She jumped.

"Wha...., oh..., it's you, Alex, I thought." She sat up and scratched the top of her head, then looked at Alex. "Where are we?" she said, standing up and looking around.

"We are still in the same place."

"Oh..., you were sitting next to me and then you passed out, so I went to walk towards Gia and...," She pointed at the ground. "I guess we should head back then."

"No! We can't!"

"But why?"

"There's something we have to do. Someone we have to see."

"Who?"

"Scathach."

"Scathach?"

"The Shadow, The Warrior."

"What?? Why do we need to see a warrior for?"

"You will see when we get there."

"Ok, do we use our crystals again?"

"Yes."

"Ok..., now?" Elsie sighed and brushed her hair back from her eyes.

"Yes, now." They held out the crystals and they started to glow brown, white, red and blue, brown, white, red then blue. A mist developed around them, brown, white, red and blue.

Alex closed his eyes tight and put his hand into his pocket. He waited and waited.

"Alex..., Alex..., we are here."

He opened his eyes and saw a large castle. They were standing on a wooden bridge in front of a large iron gate. One woman was standing in front of the gate looking down at them.

"A' hum," Alex cleared his throat, "We are here to see Scathach."

"The Shadow Warrior," stated Elsie.

"Is that right?!?" A loud female voice came from behind them. Alex and Elsie jumped.

"HAHA! Sorry if I scared ya! Are ya looking for me?"

"Are you Sca...," Alex began to say when Elsie cut him off. "Yes, Scathach Mam."

"Oh, HA! No need to call me Mam, young lady. Just Scatty will do just fine!"

"Ok, Scatty." Elsie blushed.

"So, what do ya all want with me, hey?"

"Gia sent us," said Elsie.

"Oh, the lovely Goddess Gia, well you might as well come in. It is getting very late. I will arrange a room for the both of you tonight. By the way, this is my daughter Uathach."

Scatty pointed to the woman in front of the gate. Alex and Elsie waved as Scatty led them through the gates and into the castle. "Welcome to the Fortress of Shadows on the Isle of Skye. Have you been on this Island before?"

"We are on an Island?" asked Alex.

"Well yes, of course you are. Didn't you notice when you hopped off your boat?" she laughed.

"Uhh..., we, we didn't come here by boat," replied Alex.

"You didn't? Then how did you get here? Flew?"

"Uh, no, we got here by this." Alex held up his pebble.

"Hmmm, very interesting. Usually, you need something..., oh doesn't matter, let's eat. I'm starving," she said, leading them into a large dining room where there were big medals and portrait's hanging around the room and a very long wooden table in the centre, piled with all types of food.

They sat down at the table and began to eat. Alex realised he was starving. He reached for a plate of potatoes and noticed that Scatty wasn't eating anything.

"I thought you were hungry," said Alex, as he put a spoon full of potatoes onto his plate.

"Oh, I don't eat food."

"Then what do you eat?"

"You really don't want to know. I'll be right back," said Scatty, walking out of the room.

Alex ate most of his dinner when suddenly Uathach ran in and yelled out, "The castle! The castle is under attack!"

Alex saw Scatty's head peek around the corner and say, "Excellent! Just in time for dinner!" Then Scatty and Uathach ran out of the room.

"I'm not sure I want to know what she eats," said Alex.

"Who's attacking?" asked Elsie, as she walked over to the window. Alex walked over to the window as well and looked out. "Oh no." There was a vast mass of sea creatures crawling, slithering, galloping, walking, running, swarming out of the sea and heading straight towards the castle.

"I've only ever seen these creatures in Books," said Alex.

"Oh, I've seen them. They are wicked beasts that can bite, sting, scratch, kick, punch and spit acid at you. Some will just eat you whole...,"

"Ok, ok, I get the drift. I'm going to have a better look," Alex said, walking over to a large telescope, wheeling it over to the window and looked into it. "Hey look!" He pointed to the creatures and continued, "Look on top of the beasts..., they are not that noticeable, but when you look really closely, you can see them."

"See what?"

"Come here, look closely."

Elsie walked over and put her eye to the telescope.

"See? Do you see them?"

"What am I supposed to be looking at?"

"Look on top of the creatures, look really carefully."

"It' s...., it's..., oh my.... IT'S SIM!" She looked at Alex and said, "And he has brought all the gnomes with him! And they are all armed with bows and arrows! What are we to do?"

"Shh..., look," he said, still looking out the window. "Scatty is down there and there's a creature galloping up to her." He looked into the telescope.

"It has Sim on its back," said Alex, as he turned around to see Elsie running out the door.

"Wait for me!" he yelled, as he ran as fast as he could out to the front door of the castle. From here, they could only just hear them talking.

"You can't have them," said Scatty.

"If you don't give them up, you will all die."

"So be it!" said Scatty and whistled a high pitch. She then proceeded to walk back through the gates to stand next to Alex and Elsie.

"GIVE THEM TO US! YOU WOULD BE STUPID TO REFUSE!" yelled Sim.

All of a sudden human-shaped figures were starting to emerge from the trees surrounding the castle. There was a multitude of Warriors wearing armour and carrying weapons. One woman came to the front and she looked just like Scatty.

"That's my sister Aife, my twin," she said proudly, then yelled out across the masses of creatures to her sister.

"LOOKS LIKE WE GET SEAFOOD, TONIGHT, SISTER!"

"I LOVE SEAFOOD!" yelled Aife.

Scatty turned to look at Alex and Elsie. "Please stay here. Don't move. I don't want you getting hurt. If I tell you to leave, you must immediately go straight to The Mistress and tell her what has happened, ok?"

They nodded as they watched Scatty go out to join her sister.

"SEAFOOD HERE WE COME!!!!" yelled Scatty.

"WAR!" yelled Aife.

There was a mass of humans and creatures, battling out in the open. Blood and bodies were lying on the ground. Elsie wrapped her arms around Alex and put her head against his shoulder. She started to cry.

"It. It's, it's ok Elsie," he said shaking, not knowing what to say.

"Just tell me when it's over."

"Ok."

A huge blue giant dripping with water was coming closer and closer to Scatty. It raised its hands up into the sky and a large black cloud formed above it. Lightning came from the cloud and down into the giant. Alex gasped. "What?!" asked Elsie, as she lifted her head and saw the giant right behind Scatty, Elsie ran up to the gate and yelled, "SCATTY!!!! STORM KELPIE GIANT BEHIND YOU!!!"

Scatty turned quickly and ran a barbed harpoon straight through the middle of the giant's head. She pulled it back out, and held up the harpoon to Elsie with blue blood dripping off of it and yelled out,

"MADE IT ME SELF!! BEST THING I'VE EVER HAD!!" Then she turned around and started fighting again.

Elsie ran back to Alex and wrapped her arms back around him, pushing her head into his chest, trying to hide. Alex watched as more and more sea beasts crawled out of the sea. Scatty must have been thinking the same thing as she looked up at the water edge where more and more creatures seemed to be just spilling out of the ocean and onto the battlefield. Scatty looked over to Alex and yelled, "YOU HAVE TO GO! GO NOW!"

"Elsie, Elsie we have to go," said Alex, looking down at her and removing her hands from her ears. "We have to go," he said once again, as she looked up at him. Elsie nodded and they held their crystals in their hands. The crystals started to light up and Alex's pocket started to vibrate again. He took one more look up at Scatty and saw a huge beast on top of her with its teeth out and saliva hanging down from its large teeth. Scatty looked like she was trying to kiss it, but he then realised that there was some sort of mist coming from around the monster and then into Scatty's mouth. Alex couldn't believe his eyes. All of a sudden, he remembered his father giving him a Book on mythological creatures. He tried to think of where the Book had gone. When he thought of the last time he had seen it, it was at Stonehenge. He was looking at the Book sitting on the ground at Stonehenge, and his father was telling him all about the sea creatures. How they have an aura just like everyone else.

All of a sudden, everything went bright Brown, White, Red and Blue. So bright that Alex had to close his eyes very tightly because he felt that one bit of that light would blind him. He then thought about Elsie. He hoped she was ok. He reached out his arm and managed to get a hold of her. Alex pulled Elsie close to his chest, so that the light didn't hurt her eyes. The ground underneath them started to shake. He held onto Elsie as tight as he could. The light was glowing Bright Brown, White, Red, Blue, Brown, White, Red, Blue, it seemed to be going through the colours faster and faster! Brown, White, Red, Blue, Brown, White, Red, Blue, THEN BOOOM! A Bright White Light!

Alex's eyes started to hurt, and he felt like he couldn't keep them closed for much longer. The light went back to Brown, White, Red, Blue, Brown, White, Red, Blue, then they slowed Brown...., White...., Red...., Blue...., then they stopped.

Alex felt his whole body relax and he slowly let go of Elsie and collapsed to the ground.

Blink, Blink, Alex slowly blinked his eyes. All he could see was blue, blink, blink, everything was a light blue. He opened his eyes and patted over his body to see if any part of him was hurt. He was ok. He then patted his pocket, the orb was still there.

"ELSIE!" he yelled all of a sudden, sitting up and looking around.

"NOOOOOOO!" he yelled. Coming to the realisation that he was in "STONEHENGE!" He yelled, "NOOOOOOOOOO! ELSIE!!!!!!!"

He stood up trying to walk straight, but he couldn't seem to balance properly. He looked around everywhere. "ELSIE!!!, ELSIE!!!!!, ELSSSIIIEEE!!!!!"

She was nowhere to be seen, and then something on the ground caught his eye. He bent down and picked up a pebble with saga, chi, clandestine written in white on it. He put his hand into his pockets and pulled out the orb from one pocket and.., his pebble from the other. Alex looked out into the distance and said, "Elsie, where are you?" He then started looking around at the ground some more. He noticed just outside of Stonehenge there were tyre marks in the dirt... They looked a lot like..., Wagon wheels, the troop? Gypsies? Did they take Elsie? Was it a cart that was on its way to the markets? He thought of all the different type of carts that could have wheels just like that. It could have been: an animal cart? a carriage? cooking cart? Gypsy caravan? a slave cart? Alex was distraught now, "Where are you, Elsie?"

been: an animal cart? a carriage? cooking cart? Gypsy caravan? a slave cart? Alex was distraught now, "Where are you, Elsie?"

Chapter 19. Where, Oh Where Are You?

'What is that?' Alex said to himself, as he noticed something moving beside one of the large stones. As he walked slowly towards it, he realised it was the bag that Frank had given to him, except it was moving! 'Wiggle, wiggle,' he could see a small lump inside slowly wriggling its way to the opening of the bag. 'Wiggle, wiggle,' it looked like it was about to escape whatever it was. The wriggling stopped and started to move backward and forward. Alex noticed that the cord on the bag had been pulled tight and tied into a knot. He stepped closer to the bag and leaned down to pick it up. 'JUMP!' The bag jumped up in the air at Alex as he stumbled backwards tripping over a rock and landing on his bottom. He stood up quickly, wiping the dirt off his trousers, gave the bag a determined stare, then he quickly bent down and picked up the bag. "Meow." He stared at it with open eyes, then as fast as his hands could manage, he quickly pulled the knotted cord apart. "It's YOU!" he said, in breathless anticipation. It was the kitten that Alex was given at school in Humbletin. He shoved the orb back into his pocket and lifted the kitten out of the bag.

"So how did you get here?" asked Alex, as he dropped the stones into the bag. "Mcreeoowllccccc...," the kitten made a strange strangling noise, coughed a few times while scratching at his throat and sat up straight. He had a serious look on his face, opened his mouth wide and said "MMMEEEOOOOWWW!!!" The kitten's eyes were so wide that they looked like big round full moons and he immediately put his front paws over his mouth.

"Oh no," said Alex, looking down at him. "I, I don't know how to help you. It must be because we are not in Humbletin anymore. Cats don't talk where I come from." The kitten took his paws off of his mouth and let out a tiny, "Mep," and continued to stare at Alex with his large round eyes.

"Ok so, you can't talk, and I don't even know what your name is?" The kitten put his head to the side and made a shrug with his shoulders.

"Do you have a name?" The kitten shook his head as to say no. "Hmm, ok, well, I'll name you...," Alex looked at the black kitten with bright orange stripes along its sides and up its tail. He looked at the stripe that was in the middle of his head. "It kind of looks like a flame. What about the name, Flame?" he asked, looking at the kitten. The kitten seemed to look like he was smiling and nodding his head. "Ok then Flame it is!" He smiled at Flame and Flame smiled back with his tail wagging from side to side.

"So, I have to go and find Elsie. She is here somewhere. I know she is, I found her stone for Fabilchi and some tracks are leading away from here. Do you want to come with me?" The kitten nodded. "Ok, do you want to ride in the bag, on my shoulder or walk on the ground?"

"You don't really expect it to answer you, do you? You do know cats can't talk, right?" said a deep Booming voice from behind him. A dark shadow came over Alex. "I, I know that voice, WAYNE!!" yelled Alex as he spun around and looked up with a big grin on his face.

"That's right, my boy. I hope we didn't scare you too much with everyone lying down like that, even the horses! By jeepers, I've never seen anything like it! It's the worst gas storm that I have ever seen in my life! I hope you are ok. My son and daughter only just managed to wake me, and they said you had come this way. I wouldn't just leave you here, after that terrible storm. I swear it must have picked us up and carried us a fair distance. I'm amazed everyone is ok and I'm sure glad that it didn't separate any of us."

"Uh," said Alex, staring up at Wayne in confusion.

"Where did you get that bag and kitten from?"

"Well, I, I found it," said Alex, feeling bad for lying but he could not tell him the truth. He didn't think Wayne would believe the truth even if he did tell him.

"Well give it here then. It might belong to one of the troops. Not the kitten though, I would know if someone had a kitten." Wayne held his large giant hand out. The kitten jumped up onto Alex's shoulder as Alex handed the bag over to Wayne.

"So, what are your plans now, boy?" asked Wayne.

"Well, I still need to go to Professor Yen 'Niles' cottage."

"You are still welcome to continue your journey with us if you like? That's if we haven't scared you too much with the storm and all."

"Oh, yes, please, I would love to."

"You can bring the kitten with you as long as you look after it ok? Don't let it run around in the troop's caravans or bother anyone."

"Yes, Sir."

"Ok that's settled then, come back to camp, everyone has been wondering what you were doing all the way over here. I'm just glad you're ok."

As they entered the camp, Alex realised that the caravans were all still in the same place as when he had left, which was very strange because he was sure he had been gone for over a week at least.

"Alex!"

"Hey Alex, over here!" He could hear people yelling out as he got closer to a group of people sitting around a campfire.

"Alex come sit by me, love," said a really tall woman who was waving him over.

"Tabitha! Hi!" replied Alex, walking over to her.

"What took you so long?" said Jonathan, who was sitting next to her.

"Well, I.., I heard a noise over there and I thought I saw…," Alex thought for a moment and had an idea. "I thought I saw a girl, a girl with short brown hair and she was a bit taller than me, did you see her? Did she walk through here?" Alex looked around the camp, wondering if she was there.

"Yeah! She was really weird," said Sarah, who was sitting next to Jonathan. Her brown hair looked like it was glowing from the bright red and orange fire flickering in front of her. Alex gazed at her lost in thought of how beautiful she looked in the light of the fire. She looked picturesque. He then became conscious he was staring and remembered Elsie. "Did she say anything? Where did she go?"

"She was acting really strange. Like she had never seen a human before," laughed Jon.

"Oh, don't be mean Jonathan, the poor girl was obviously lost and didn't know where she was that's all," said Tabitha.

"Come sit over here next to me Alex," said Sarah. moving over to make some room on the log they were sitting on. Alex walked over and sat down. Then there was a loud 'Thump.' The ground shook. It felt like there was an earthquake, but it was just Wayne who had sat on the log opposite the fire. The logs moved in the fire making little sparks fly through the air. Alex thought that it looked quite pleasing as the sun had almost disappeared behind the mountains in the distance.

"So, what did she say?" asked Alex.

"Well another strange thing is, she said she was looking for a boy and she described a boy who looked just like you," said Tabitha.

"And?" said Alex, looking more worried.

"Well, I said the only boy we know who looks like that was you and then she asked where you were going, and I said you were on your way to Professor Yen 'Niles' cottage and she asked where that was, so I told her. I thought you had gone already. I didn't know that you had just gone for a walk until Jonathan had told me. Do you know her Alex?"

"Umm... Yes... I remember her from around my hometown."

"Oh, I am sorry dear," said Tabitha.

"It's ok you didn't know. I have to go after her. She won't know where she is," said Alex, worried.

"You can't go now, it's late and dark. You'll get cold and hungry and you just can't go now, stay the night at least," said Sarah. Alex looked into her eyes and found that he couldn't say no. "Well... Ok, just for the night," he said, feeling guilty about Elsie and how she must feel so lost and confused not knowing where she was, with everything so different here compared to Humbletin. Alex wondered for a second if Elsie might try talking to a street lamp or something and he let out a small laugh.

"What's so funny?" asked Sarah.

"Oh nothing, just happy that you are all ok, that's all."

"And we are glad that you are ok too Alex. You seem tired, you must be hungry and thirsty by now?" asked Tabitha. Alex nodded. "A bit."

"I will fix you something," said Sarah, as she reached out her delicate hand and softly brushed aside Alex's hair with her fingertips so that his hair was away from his eyes. "That's better now you can see," she giggled, stood up and walked away, disappearing into one of the caravans. Alex had this feeling come over him like he wanted to go after her. He put his hands on the log about to stand up. There was another 'Thump' and a few grumbles from the other side of the fire pit. Wayne had stood up and the other people who were sitting on the log had slid over to another giant man who was sitting on the other side of the log. Alex laughed as he watched Wayne say he was very sorry and walk off to the same caravan that Sarah had entered.

"You like her, don't you?" Alex quickly looked beside him, remembering that Jon was there.

"Uh, pardon?"

"You like her, don't you? My sister?"

"Oh..., uh...,"

"I don't mind you know. I've seen a few guys try to chat up my sister, but I never liked any of them and neither did she, but I really think she likes you and... Well... I think your...," Jon nodded slowly, not knowing what to say, "You know...?"

"Uh... Thanks... I guess...," replied Alex.

"Hey, son! Why don't you play us some music? I think we are all in need of some good hearty music. Do you have your lute there?"

"Ok mum, I've got it here." Jon turned and grabbed his lute from behind him and started playing an upbeat song and everyone started to sing along.

"I wonder what's taking Sarah so long?" Tabitha said out loud. Alex looked across the fire pit and noticed that Wayne was back sitting on the log and singing with the others.

"Do you want me to?" said Alex, pointing towards the caravan.

"If you don't mind?" asked Tabitha.

Alex nodded. "Sure..., ok...," he said standing up. He felt a little nervous knowing that he would be alone with Sarah for the first time. He brushed off his clothes and tried to neaten his hair as he walked over to the caravan.

When he stepped inside the caravan, there was a whistling noise that seemed to be coming from behind the see-through red curtain with gold triangles which were parting off the back of the caravan. He could see Sarah's figure standing behind the curtain. Alex started to feel uncomfortable and the palms of his hands were sweating. He rubbed them together, tried to relax his neck moving his head side to side and then let out a little cough. He saw her jump a little. "Who's there?" she said, then peeked through the curtain. "Oh, it's just you, Alex."

"Sorry if I frightened you."

"Just startled me that's all, have a seat. I was just finishing making you a cup of tea."

"Uh, ok." Alex looked around him noticing that there were chairs and tables. He sat at a table.

"Sorry it's taken me so long. I had to heat up your dinner that's all. It's heated up now."

Alex let out another little cough feeling like his throat was restricted. "That's (cough) ok."

Sarah walked out holding a tray with a bowl of what looked like tomato soup, some buttered bread and a mug of tea.

"Here you go, I hope it's hot enough," said Sarah, sitting at the table opposite him.

"You're (cough) not having any? (cough)."

"No, no, I'm fine," she said smiling at him.

Alex picked up a spoon and started to eat his soup.

"Nice?"

"Mmm yes very nice, thank you," he said, going a bit red in the face while trying to concentrate on eating his soup without spilling it all over himself. His hands were shaking from being so nervous.

"I made it myself. I love to cook. I hope one day I will even own my own cafe, nothing big of course just a little one. Then I can share my food with everyone. That would be great, that's my dream anyway. Do you have any dreams, Alex?"

Alex thought about the few unusual dreams he had while he was in Humbletin, then remembered that he had dreamed of her at least twice. He went red in the face again. "Uh, not really," he said, then continued to eat. "Aww that's sad, I think everyone should have dreams. As they say, you should dream and dream big, for one day, your dreams may just come true."

Sarah sighed and said, "But that's ok, you can share my dream." She giggled. "I don't mind sharing." Alex let out a small breath 'ha' just as he was about to put the spoon in his mouth and the tomato soup splattered onto his shirt.

"Oh no, I'm sorry. I shouldn't be speaking while you are trying to eat, let me get a cloth." She walked off into the kitchen. Alex took the time to sit up and take a deep breath. He could hear the lute playing outside and people talking and laughing.

"Here you go," said Sarah, as she walked back out holding a yellow cloth. She walked over to him and started to dab his shirt with the cloth.

"So, uh, everyone is ok from what happened?"

"Oh yes everyone is ok. There we go, all clean again," she said, then walked back out behind the curtain.

Alex felt his eyes getting a little sore. He sat there, listening to the music that was playing outside. It sounded like Jon was now playing a slow song, or was he just playing around with the lute? Because it seemed to have no rhythm like he was trying to play a song in reverse, it almost sounded like the strings on the lute was out of tune.

He looked back at his dinner and thought he had eaten most of it and wondered if Sarah would take offence if he didn't ea..t... He continued to stare at the bowl and thought, is that bowl moving or... No... It... then the room started to get blurry. "Sa...ra...," he managed to whisper then everything went black.

When Alex awoke his head was aching and he felt sick. He could feel something brushing his hair. He slowly sat up and sitting next to him was Sarah, stroking his hair with a worried look on her face.

"Wh.., what happened?" asked Alex.

"You just passed out. I was so worried about leaving you here, so I slept on the couch over there to keep an eye on you. I woke up not that long ago as well. I'm going to go get dad. He will probably get our doc to see you just in case."

Alex nodded, leaning his elbows on the table and putting his face in his hands.

About five minutes later Sarah came back in.

"I couldn't find dad, but the doctor will be here soon, I will make you a cup of tea." She walked into the kitchen and put the kettle on the stove.

"Meeoow, Meow Meoow." Flame jumped up the steps and ran up to Alex. "What? What is it?"

"Meeowwwwww."

"That's right you can't talk," said Alex, as Sarah walked out of the kitchen laughing. "Of course a cat can't talk Alex ha!"

Alex stood up and looked down at Flame. "What is it, boy? Flame ran to the door then back to Alex. "Uh sorry I've got to go Sarah," said Alex, as he rushed out of the caravan after Flame.

"Wait!" He could hear Sarah yell as he almost fell down the steps. Flame ran across the other side of the camp and into another caravan where there was a large bed. On top of the bed was Alex's bag. He picked up the bag and tipped it upside down. The old clothing that Elsie's father had given him had fallen onto the bed. Alex picked up the few pieces of clothing one by one. "They're gone!" The next second Sarah came running in. "Wait," she said, trying to catch her breath. Alex looked at Sarah not knowing what to say. He watched her as she fell back onto the bed sitting forward holding her chest.

"Do, do you know something about this?" asked Alex.

"I."

"Is that why I blacked out last night?"
"Well, I."

"What have they done?"

"Just, hold on a second," said Sarah, still trying to catch her breath. Alex sat down on the bed and looked at her.

Sarah looked at him and said, "Ok, yes."

"What? You knocked me out last night?!?"

"Yes, I mean no."

"Well, which is it?"

"I didn't knock you out."

"Then how did I blackout?"

"I, well, Dad, dad came in to see me last night when I was making your dinner and he gave me something he said would make you sleepy."

"But why?"

"You see there's something you don't know about us, me, dad, mum and Jon and a few other people you don't know."

"And? Why did they take my things?"

"They aren't yours."

"What do you mean they aren't mine?"

"It's a long story, Alex. Can we please go back and sit down? I have the kettle on, and I don't want it to boil over."

Alex nodded and followed Sarah back into the other caravan where she made them both a cup of tea and put a small crystal bowl of milk on the floor for Flame.

Alex and Sarah sat across from one another.

"Alright, I guess I better tell you from the start. I know what you were looking for, the stones, am I right?" Alex nodded. "Ok, well, they are not really yours because they are mum and dads."

"How? I never took them from here."

"I know, however, they were originally mum and dads. You see, they created them in the first place. The stones are ancient and they go back to when there were no houses at all, only caves and, well, I don't think you're going to believe me."

"Trust me I have seen a lot of things that I would not have believed a few weeks ago, or was it yesterday? The day before? I'm so confused, but please just tell me I think I could believe anything right about now."

"HaHa, well ok then. You see I'm not really, what, or who, you think I am."

"What do you mean?"

"Do you remember me telling you what age I am?"

"Yeah?"

"I'm a lot older than you think I am."

"You don't look it."

"I was born over 500 years ago."

Alex's eyes widened. "What? That would make you?"

"Old," she laughed. Alex nodded.

"You know, I don't even know how old I am anymore. I got to 510 then I stopped counting."

"You're right when you said it would be hard for me to believe," said Alex.

"Well, that's not even all of it."

"There's more?"

"Yep, you see mum and dad lived in a cave and mum's kind of, a, what you would call a witch."

"A witch?"

"Back then they were called Mystics, anyway, mum enchanted the stones and dad helped her to shape and write on them. They had one each."

"What did they use them for?"

"They are teleportation stones. When you hold them and think of where you want to go you will be there. Mum said that dad did use to use his a lot when he would go out hunting with the other giants so that he could teleport everyone back home, so they didn't get lost. Oh, and back then there were creatures like you have never seen, so it was very dangerous to go out of your home."

"Wow," said Alex, looking amazed as he stroked Flame who was now sitting on the corner of the table.

"Yeah, mum has told me all about it. She said that they had a huge cave that had stone stairs going up to the top of the mountain and it had all different rooms in it. There was one huge room that they called the hatchery, and it was full of straw nests and inside the nests were dragon eggs."

"Ohh wow, did you get to see dragons?"

"Uh, no, unfortunately not. One day mum and dad went outside of the grounds with a few of their friends to go hunting and mum was going to go foraging and well… they forgot the stones. Mum says ever since that day they've never been back home."

"So why are you not a giant like them?"

"I wondered that for a while when I was growing up, so one day I asked mum and she said it's because I was born here outside of the caves. Jon is the same. At first, mum was so worried that we were humans and that we would die, so she kept a close eye on us every day to see how fast we were growing. Mum said she thinks it's because we have some of her magic inside of us and that's why we don't age as humans do."

"So, uh, does that mean, that, that they have gone back?"

"Yes, Jon went with them too."

"But, but what about you?? What if they can't come back? Why didn't you go?"

"I was thinking about it and, well I looked at you collapsed on the table all alone and, well, I didn't want you waking up and not knowing what had happened and, and well, I might not have been able to see you ever again, so… well, I chose to stay with you." Alex stared at her then said, "What? Are you insane?! That is your family!"

Sarah jumped a little at his response. She could not understand why he was reacting in this way. She thought he would be happy. Alex became aware that she was startled and said, "Sorry, I didn't mean to yell like that, but that's your family and I know what it's like to lose your family."

"I know Alex. I just felt like it wasn't my time yet. I want to help you, anyway I know they will come back for me."

"Elsie!" said Alex, sitting up straight. "I've got to find her. She doesn't know this place."

"Who is she?"

"It's another long story, but It will have to wait. I have to find her!"

"Then I'm coming with you."

"You don't need to come with me."

"I want to."

"Ok, you better go pack some clothes quickly."

"I'll grab us some food and water as well."

"And I'll go get my bag and clothes."

"Ok, see you back here."

"Alright," replied Alex.

Walking over the rolling hills, Sarah looked at Alex and asked, "Do you even know where you're going?"

"I think I do. It's been a long time since I've been to Professor Yen 'Niles' Cottage. Was I really only gone for one day?"

"Yes, it's the power of the stones. They take you to whatever place and time you want to be in. You must have been thinking about getting back to your father or something."

"To tell you the truth, I haven't stopped thinking about it. I just want to get home to my family. I wish I had never come here in the first place."

"But then you wouldn't have met our troop and me."

"Yeah, I suppose that's true too." Flame let out a "Meow."

"Yes, and you too Flame and Elsie, Actually I wouldn't change a thing. I am glad that I have met every single one of you."

Flame ran in front of Alex and stood up on his back legs reaching up to Alex. "Come here you," said Alex, as he reached down, picked him up, put him on his shoulder and continued to walk.

"Hey, what's that," said Sarah, pointing to something small lying on the ground under a tree.

"It looks like clothes or…,"

"I think it's a child," said Sarah, as they walked closer.

"No, it's… Elsie!" yelled Alex as he ran up to the body lying under the tree. "Elsie! Elsie!" yelled Alex as he shook her trying to wake her. Elsie rolled over and mumbled something under her breath.

"She has nothing, no water or food or anything, here take these," said Sarah, as she handed him a large bottle of water and a sandwich. Alex put the water to Elsie's lips, and she took a tiny sip. "Drink, please drink," said Alex, looking worried. He put his hand under her neck, and she sat up a little, taking sips of the water.

"Are you ok Elsie?" asked Sarah. Elsie nodded her head a little.

"Can you talk?" asked Alex.

"Ye, yes."

"What happened?"

"I just, I."

"I think she is just dehydrated, drink up Elsie and have something to eat," said Sarah. Elsie nodded.

Sarah whispered into Alex's ear, "Does she come from here?"

"What do you mean?"

"Does she live here, or did she come from somewhere else?"

"She comes from Humbletin."

"Where's that?"

"I don't know. It's someplace I was transported to from Stonehenge."

"Damn it."

"What?"

"It's not good news, I'm sorry to say."

"What? What's not?"

"She can't stay here, Alex. Every minute she stays in our world her energy will fade and she will get very sick until...,"

"Until what?"

"Well... until she...,"

"NO!" yelled Alex as he went and sat next to Elsie and held her hand. Elsie looked up at him. "What? What's wrong?" she struggled to say.

"We, we have to get you to professor Yen 'Niles'."

"Why?"

"You need a rest, that's all."

Elsie nodded and with the help of Alex she slowly stood up and put her arm around his shoulders for support.

"We are nearly there anyway. It's just over there near those hedges." Alex pointed to a line of green, purple and dark red hedges. As they walked closer, they could see a yard full of flowering trees, herb gardens, roses and all sorts of plants, even some that Alex had never seen before.

Chapter 20. The Parting

'KNOCK, KNOCK.' Alex knocked on the front door of a small wooden cottage.

"Just a minute!" yelled out a deep husky voice. A couple of minutes later, the door opened a tiny bit with a 'screech.' "Oh, it's just you, Alex," said the man behind the door. "Come in." The three of them stumbled into the old man's cottage. "Have a seat," he said, gesturing to the soft brown couches that sat opposite each other. "Oh no, Alex what have you done," said the old man, as he rushed over to Elsie. His long grey hair and beard were swaying from side to side. "What have you done?" He looked up at Alex while helping Elsie onto a couch. "Uh, I, I don't know what you mean Sir."

"Where did you find this girl?"

"Well. It's kind of a long story."

"Humbletin?"

Alex looked at the old man with surprise.

"I wasn't born yesterday, Alex, as you might realise."

"Yes, Sir."

"She needs to go home and as soon as possible!"

Elsie looked up at Alex, her eyes were going red and her face was going a shade of white. "Allleexx...," She said slowly. "Do you have it, boy?"

"Wha… oh yes." He flung his hand into his pocket and pulled out the orb. The old man grabbed the orb and held it tightly in his hands. "If you want to say goodbye do it and Quickly!!" Alex ran over to Elsie's side and wrapped his arms around her. "I don't want you to leave."

"I know," said Elsie softly. "But you have to and… there's so much more I want to say to you." Elsie nodded and whispered something into Alex's ear. Alex grinned and Elsie kissed him on the cheek. The man started chanting words that Alex had never heard before. The orb began glowing bright colours, Red, Brown, White, Blue and Elsie faded away like a ghost into the night.

"Professor!" said Sarah, as the old man collapsed onto one of the cushioned couches. "I'll get you some water." She ran into the kitchen, filled a cup with water from the sink and gave it to the old man. He grabbed the cup. The long white sleeves of his robes dangled over the arms of the couch as he took a sip of water. He leaned back with an, "Ah… that's better."

"Are you ok Professor Yen 'Nile?" asked Alex.

The Professor nodded.

"What will happen to Elsie?"

"She will be back home where she belongs."

"How do you know?"

"We met a long time ago. She probably doesn't remember. She was only a little baby and her brother, oh boy, was he a mischief-maker."

"He still is," laughed Alex, "and he is in scouts."

The old man laughed out loud. The toes of his blue pointed shoes jumped up and down as he laughed. "That boy, a scout! They are in for so much trouble."

"That's for sure."

"Oh, and Hi Sarah, so good to see you again."

"Again? You've met before?"

Sarah nodded. "A few times while we were travelling, we would stop here and get some herbal remedies from the Professor."

"How is your Troop?"

Sarah looked down at her knees. "I, I let them go without me. I couldn't leave Alex that way. I didn't want him thinking that we had done something bad."

"I understand."

"You know about that too?" asked Alex.

"I know a good lot of things. That's one reason why they want to get their hands on me."

"Who does?"

"The other side."

"The other side?"

"After all you have been through so far, Alex, you still don't know about the other side?"

"Umm...," replied Alex, not knowing what to say. Sarah shook her head. Professor Yen 'Nile looked at her, surprised. "Really?"

"He hasn't said anything about them," replied Sarah.

"Ok well sit and listen, Alex."

Alex nodded and sat down.

"When the first magic started, which was in the same era as Sarah's mother and father, there was one man who stood out from everyone else. His name was Monsuma. He was a great Voodoo Shaman. He had deep, dark skin. You could almost see your refection shinning off his skin. His hair was black as ink, mattered together like snakes. He wore platted hair around his wrists from women who admired him. It was the way a woman showed their interest in a man in those days. Most men received one or two. However, Monsuma had more than anyone. Some people thought that he had put love spells on the women for attention because he wanted to be loved more than any man. Then, one day he vanished. No one could find him anywhere. They even had a hunting horde go out and search for him. He was nowhere to be seen. Then a couple of days later people started to die."

"Sarah, if this is too much for you to hear we can go somewhere else if you like?"

"No, it's fine, I wasn't there, and I would like to hear what happened please."

"Ok, no problem just let me know if it's getting too much for you." Sarah nodded. "Where was I? Oh yes then people started to mysteriously die. No one could figure out what had happened to them. The first day we just thought maybe it was a flu or something, then the next morning many women did not wake up. That's when they realised that it was only women and the only connection they had was Monsuma."

"Then what happened?" asked Sarah.

"Well I'm not sure you know about this part Sarah, but your parents went out looking for him."

"What??"

"Yes, that's right. That's how your mother and father ended up here."

"But mum told me they went out for food."

"Maybe she didn't think it was the right time to tell you yet. However, they were very brave to go hunting for Monsuma. Your mother and father didn't want anyone else getting hurt. If they didn't do what they did, we would not know about the dark side and we would not be able to protect ourselves from them now.

Monsuma had come to our world and started to recruit people to join him in his Black Voodoo Rituals. Soon enough he had followers that were completely and utterly dedicated to him. Of course, some died along the way, but he didn't care, he would just replace them. They are in this world and in other worlds even in Humbletin."

"I think I saw some of them before I got back. They were evil and full of rage."

"Yes, most of them are changelings and they can form into humans whenever they like, but their natural forms are beastly. By the way, Alex, where is your watch? The one that your grandfather had given to you?"

"Umm... Well... there was a man in a boat and the only way he would take me across the water was for payment and I had no money and...,"

"Uhh yes... that's ok, was it a man with a scar on his face?"

"Yes, he took my watch for payment."

"Don't worry, you will get it back. He is one of us."

"Thank God, my father would have killed me."

"About that, you better not tell your father that you went into Stonehenge ok?"

"Does dad know about it? He made that thing, that, that orb, how, how?" stammered Alex.

"Your father is a great man. He can do things that no other man has done before. That is why you need to understand this Alex, because of this, all of your family is in great danger. Your father sent you to me on purpose. I am to explain everything to you and your mother doesn't know much about what is going on. She only knows that Stonehenge is a mysterious place because something happened a very long time ago when you were only a little child. Do you remember anything at all about Stonehenge from when you were young, Alex?"

"No, I don't, but when I was there, I felt sad and I had these strange feelings. That doesn't happen to everyone, does it, Professor?"

"No, it doesn't."

"It was the orb that sent me to Humbletin, wasn't it?"

"Yes, that's right and the feelings you felt, there is a reason."

"There is?"

"When you were a small child Alex, you had a brother."

"What?!?"

"Yes, you had a brother. He was just like you. You were twins, not identical, but you were both born on the same day at the same time."

"Where is he?" asked Alex, as images started to form in his mind of a little boy playing hide and seek.

"I think you know deep down, don't you?"

Alex started to have more images flowing into his mind of his mother and father sitting on a red and white checked cloth on the ground inside Stonehenge. They looked like they were having a picnic. There was a light cane basket with buns inside and a little boy was playing with his dad. "Dad?" It was like he was there with them watching two little boys, almost identical, running around and playing hide and seek. Then one of the boys went behind a large stone and the other boy, which Alex now realised was himself, went to jump behind the stone and the other boy was gone. The boy laughed and thought his brother had just run behind another stone, so he ran around all the stones saying, "BOO!" And each time he did this there was a sad look on the little boy's face. Then their mother looked up and yelled out, "Boys time for lunch!" Little Alex ran up to his mum and mumbled something that his mother could not understand. His mother then sang out, "Josh stop being silly, come get lunch!" She suddenly stood up and looked around all the stones.

"Will! I can't find him!" His father then stood up and started looking as well. Little Alex was sitting down on the cloth, rocking backwards and forwards crying.

"You remembered, didn't you? Came a deep husky voice over his parents calling out for his brother Josh.

"Whuh, uh, uhha."

"You know now, don't you?"

"Josh…?"

"Yes, you had a brother named Josh."

"I…. I remember."

"Did you see what your father was wearing that day?"

"Uhh… He had a white shirt…,"

"What was on it? as a matter of fact, what was hanging out of his pocket?"

Alex closed his eyes and tried to remember. "Granddads watch!!!!" he yelled out, opening his eyes. Professor Yen 'Nile nodded, "Indeed."

"What, what does that mean?"

"You see this?" He held out the orb in front of Alex "Yeah."

"Well that watch does the same thing. Your father didn't know, you see, that watch was left to your father before your grandfather had a chance to explain anything to your father. Your grandfather had the same gift as your father does. The gift is handed down in the family passing through blood, from father to son. Alex remembered Josh in Humbletin and how he liked to create things and said quietly, "My brother."

"Anyway, my boy, it is time that you headed home. Say hello to your mother and father for me."

"Goodbye, Alex, I will come and visit you sometime," said Sarah, kissing him on the cheek and giving him a big hug.

"Bye Sarah, I hope I see you again."

"You will."

Professor Yen 'Nile stood in front of Alex holding the orb tightly in his hands. "Saga Chi Clandestine, Saga, Chi Clandestine!" The room went bright, and he closed his eyes. Alex opened his eyes. It was night, and he was standing at the front of his house. "I'm home!" he shouted. The front porch light came on and his mother came running out of the house, wrapping her arms around him. "I've missed you, my son."

"I missed you too mum, where's Father?"

Alex looked up as he noticed a man standing in the doorway. "Father?"

"Yes, it's me, son," said a deep, loud voice.

As his father began to walk closer to him, Alex became aware that he no longer looked like an old and wrinkled man, but now was clean-shaven, had short hair and looked half his age. "Dad you look...,"

"It's ok, it's still me," he laughed, "It's amazing what a good shower and shave can do for a man." William had a broad bright smile with bright white teeth.

"Meowwww."

"Oh, Flame!!" Alex bent down and picked up his kitten.

"So, who is this little one?" asked his mother.

"This is Flame, can I keep him please?"

"You sure can son," said his father and patted the kitten on the head as Flame began to purr loudly.

"Let's go inside. I bet you are starving Hunny," said his mother.

"Yes please, we are both starving."

"Meow."

"I have so much I want to tell you. I missed you both so much." Alex, Flame, his mother and father all walked inside, Alex was home at last.

THE END.

www.ingramcontent.com/pod-product-compliance
Lightning Source LLC
Chambersburg PA
CBHW061058100726
47911CB00012B/296